All Together Now

MONICA McINERNEY

PAN BOOKS

First published 2008 by Penguin Australia

This edition published 2009 by Pan Books
an imprint of Pan Macmillan Ltd
Pan Macmillan, 20 New Wharf Road, London N1 9RR
Basingstoke and Oxford
Associated companies throughout the world
www.panmacmillan.com

ISBN 978-0-230-74205-5

1 3 5 7 9 8 6 4 2

A CIP catalogue record for this book is available from
the British Library.

Printed and bound in the UK by CPI Mackays, Chatham ME5 8TD

Visit www.panmacmillan.com to read more about all our books
and to buy them. You will also find features, author interviews and
news of any author events, and you can sign up for e-newsletters
so that you're always first to hear about our new releases.

For my dear friend and
wise mentor, Max Fatchen,
with love and thanks

Acknowledgements

'Hippy Hippy Shake' first appeared in *For Me* (1998); 'Spellbound' first appeared in *Woman's Day* (1999); 'Just Desserts' first appeared in *Girls Night In 2, Gentlemen by Invitation* (Penguin Australia, 2001); 'Sweet Charity' first appeared in *Sunset: Penguin Australian Summer Stories* (Penguin Australia, 2005); 'The Long Way Home' first appeared in *Girls Night In 4* (Penguin Australia, 2005); 'The Role Model' is original to this collection; 'Wedding Fever', written for this collection, also appeared in *Australian Women's Weekly* (October 2008); *Odd One Out* was originally published for the 2006 Books Alive campaign.

Contents

Introduction

I was eight years old when I wrote my first story, the tale of a family called the Smiths who travel to Perth on a train. After great deliberation, I called it 'The Smith Family Goes to Perth on the Train'. Thirty-five years later I've realized two things about my writing: one, I don't need to sum up the entire plot in the title and, two, I'm still intrigued by the same themes – families and the journeys they take, physically and emotionally.

I'm sure I have my childhood to blame. I grew up as the middle child in a family of nine, in what I'd call a cauldron of words. Every day brought drama, laughter and entertainment, all the ingredients I now like to include in my writing.

The stories in this collection were written over the past ten years, for magazines, anthologies and the Books Alive reading campaign, as well as two new stories especially for this book. Gathering them together has been like looking back through a photo album. I can remember where I was when I wrote each one, what idea sparked the story, what was happening in my life, even where the names of characters came from.

A sighting of a girl in full Goth regalia walking beside a make-up-free girl led to 'Hippy Hippy Shake'. I bought a box of secondhand books in a market one day and found an old book of household tips buried at the bottom. 'Spellbound' was written around that time. An article in a magazine about food trends sparked 'Just Desserts'. I wrote 'Sweet Charity' because I had just finished my fourth novel, *The Alphabet Sisters*, and wasn't ready to say goodbye to Lola, the fearless and fashion-challenged grandmother at the heart of the story.

Living in Dublin, I often see tour parties around the city. A group of young, happy travellers caught my eye one afternoon. At the back was an older, sadder woman, who seemed apart from the others. I couldn't get her face out of my mind. 'The Long Way Home' was written for her.

'Wedding Fever' came from a neighbour telling me guiltily she'd hired a cleaning lady, and had been up all night scrubbing the house before her arrival. 'The Role Model' was sparked by friends joining a weight-loss group and changing, physically and emotionally, before my eyes.

I wrote my novella 'Odd One Out' after seeing a magazine story about a family of artists and painters, illustrated with a glamorous photo of the parents and three beautiful daughters around a table. The caption mentioned casually that there was a fourth daughter who wasn't pictured. The story of Sylvie, the 'invisible' daughter, started to take shape that same day.

Although each of these stories is very different, they all touch on subjects close to my heart: family, friendship, love, travel and adventure. It's the everyday dilemmas of life that intrigue me, the choices we all face, the mistakes we make, our yearning for happiness and understanding.

I'm delighted to bring my stories between two covers for the first time and I hope you enjoy them all.

Warmest wishes and happy reading,

Monica McInerney
Dublin

Hippy Hippy Shake

Dee's cheery greeting to her sister came to an abrupt stop as the front door of the flat slowly opened.

Before her was a figure sporting long, tangled hair, multi-coloured layers of beads, bells and scarves and a fringed skirt edged in grass and leaves. A cloud of incense and the odour of aromatic oils wafted around her.

Last week her sister had looked like one of the Spice Girls. Now she was more like the Herb Queen.

'Liz?' Dee squeaked. 'Is that you? What on earth's happened? Why are you wearing that costume?'

Liz gave her older sister a beatific smile. 'It's not a costume, Dee, and please don't call me "Liz". After tonight's renaming ceremony I'll only answer to my new name.'

What new name? Dee thought. And what naming ceremony? She thought she'd been invited over for a flat-warming dinner . . . 'What *is* your new name?'

'Waveflow,' Liz answered, serenely.

Dee made a strange noise. 'Waveflow,' she said slowly. 'Uh huh. And what do I call you for short, "Wave" or "Flow"?' she asked, failing to control her grin.

Liz was unmoved. 'By poking fun at others you are expressing your own unhappiness with the world, Dee. I seek a life in harmony with nature and the elements and my new name reflects that. I ask you to respect it.'

How can I respect a name that sounds like a new toilet cleaner? Dee thought. Still, better go along with it for the moment, she decided. It couldn't be worse than Liz's last craze as a Trekkie, when you couldn't move in her bedroom without bumping against objects wrapped in silver foil and models of space ships suspended from the ceiling. Or the time last year when Liz had suddenly become horse-mad. For a month she'd worn nothing but jodhpurs and riding boots and talked incessantly about gymkhanas and dressage competitions – despite the fact she'd never even ridden a horse.

Following her sister into the kitchen, Dee winced at the smell of incense and oils. Reluctantly, she accepted a glass of dandelion wine, thinking longingly of the bottle of champagne she'd brought over.

'I'm ready to begin the ceremony when you are, Dee,' Liz said, moving a tall candle onto the table.

'Oh, I'm more than ready,' Dee said, gagging at the taste of the wine. Ready to call the funny farm, she thought.

Eyes shut, Liz lowered herself to the hessian mat on the floor, took a slow, deep breath and began to move her arms in a swaying movement in front of her, whispering 'Waveflow' over and over again.

It was going to be a long night. Dee sighed, looking around the room for clues to this latest, sudden character transformation.

Her sister's flat was in the basement of a rambling old house owned by their cousins, who had always lived what their parents called an 'alternative' lifestyle. Alternative and contagious, Dee thought.

Dee took advantage of Liz's sudden trance to cast an eye over her CD collection. There wasn't a pop singer in sight. Instead the shelf was filled with dolphin cries, natural bush sounds and one promising the 'gentle lapping of the Mediterranean Sea on a still moonlit night'. 'As if the Mediterranean sounds different to any other sea,' Dee muttered, startling Liz from her trance. 'You do know all these effects are done on a synthesiser, Liz, don't you?'

'That's your perception, Dee. Nature's sounds have their own music, whatever the delivery process, and through that they soothe my soul and release my inner creativity . . .'

Dee snapped. 'Soothe your soul? Creativity? How can the sound of three bison rooting through some undergrowth inspire creativity? You'd be better off buying a weekly pass to the zoo – at least you'd get to see the animals!'

Liz ignored her, returning to her chanting. Dee opted for a more direct approach.

'Liz, you're thirty years old – it's time to put these fads behind you. Look at yourself. For heaven's sake, your hair looks like it hasn't been combed in days.'

'It hasn't,' Liz said. 'Combing the hair strips the body of a protective circle of electricity that —'

'All right, all right. But what about your clothes? And those earrings – you look like you've just lost a fight in a chicken shed.'

'They are not earrings, Dee, they are miniature dream catchers based on an ancient Indian tradition —'

'Liz, I'm sorry, but this time I think you've gone too far. Quite frankly, I'd be embarrassed to walk down the street with you.'

With that, Dee stalked down the hall towards the front door. As she fumbled in her bag for her car keys, she caught sight of herself in the wall mirror. With a practised hand she fluffed up her orange Mohawk, reapplied her black lipstick and adjusted her razor-blade nose-ring.

Be seen with a hippy? No way. A girl had to have some self-respect.

Spellbound

Lucy stomped into the living room, slamming the door behind her.

'Never again, Jill. If you ever hear me say the words "Internet dating" again, lock me in a cupboard and never let me out.'

Jill looked up calmly from the floor, where she was sitting unpacking a box of books.

Lucy was in a right state. 'Forget blind dates, speed dating, matchmaking, all of them!'

'He was that bad?'

'Worse. There must have been a virus in the computer when they matched us up. He was a beer-swilling, football-mad, leering, belching chauvinist pig. I had to escape through the back door of the restaurant. He's probably still there, balancing empty glasses on his head by now. I'll just have to face facts, I'm going to be on my own for the rest of my life.'

Jill reached up and patted her sister affectionately. 'You just have to be patient. You know what Mum says, every pot has its lid.'

'Oh, sure. It's all right for you, you've had Tom following you around adoringly since you were in primary school. I'm nearly thirty, Jill, I'm getting desperate. I haven't met a decent man in years. The only way I'll ever get a man to fall in love with me is through hypnosis or witchcraft.'

'Well, this will get you started then,' Jill grinned, holding up an old notebook covered in peeling brown paper. 'I found it with these books I bought at the garage sale on Sunday.'

Lucy read the spidery handwriting on the cover. ' "Wizard's Tips". What is it, a book of spells?'

'It's hard to tell, half the pages are falling to bits. It's got everything from how to use honey to heal wounds to guessing the date by looking at the moon.'

'Sounds more like handy household hints than witchcraft,' Lucy said, still in a grumpy mood after her disappointing night.

'Come on, you're the one who said you were desperate. I'm sure I saw something in here about finding love. Here it is – the page is a bit ripped but it sounds like just what you need: "How to attract love".'

Lucy threw herself onto the couch in a dramatic move-ment. 'What do I have to do, catch frogs and swallow them whole?'

Jill read slowly, having difficulty with the faded handwriting. 'It sounds much nicer than that. "Carefully prepare a bed of earth close to your home, choose a favoured selection of flower seedlings, plant in a row representing . . ." It's hard to read, something about sowing them in the shape of your name ". . . to face the sunshine. Talk to them each morning, sprinkle with scented rose water and treat gently."' Jill looked up. 'Well, it certainly sounds romantic.'

'It could be my last chance,' Lucy sighed dramatically.

By the time Jill came out next morning for her breakfast, Lucy had made a shopping list of spell ingredients.

'Don't look so surprised – I told you I was desperate. I'll go to that new garden centre near work at lunchtime. At least it will keep me out of singles' bars for a while.'

When Jill arrived home from work Lucy was on her knees in the front garden, surrounded by compost, rose water and dozens of seedlings. She grinned sheepishly.

'We couldn't work out exactly which flowers the spell was referring to, so we decided to go for one of each variety.'

'Who's we?'

'Robert Kelly, do you remember him from school? I hadn't seen him in years. He's back from overseas and working in the garden store. He was really helpful.'

By the first week the entire front garden bed had been lovingly dug and prepared, and all the flower seedlings planted.

'The book said plant them in the pattern of a name, but I bought so many seedlings I've spelt out my name, your name, your Tom's name and Mum and Dad's names.' Lucy was very animated. 'I've decided to get something else going as well, while I wait for the spell to work. Robert reckons now's the right time to plant summer vegetables too. I may as well dig up that side bed. It's full of weeds at the moment.'

A week later, the side garden was transformed.

'There are tomatoes, beans and corn coming along now. Robert says I should also think about a few herbs, they keep the insects away, he says, and they'll be great for cooking too.'

Another week passed. 'Jill, do you want to keep those old daisies around the tank at the back? It's just that Robert suggested a new variety of ivy that looks brilliant growing up the side of tanks.'

Nearly five weeks had gone by before Jill realised she hadn't heard Lucy bemoan her lack of boyfriends for ages. In fact, she wasn't bemoaning anything much at all. Every spare minute she had she was in the garden digging and planting, or at the garden store trying to decide what to dig or plant next.

Robert had started to call around to lend a hand. In the fifteen years since Jill had last seen him he had grown from a gangly teenager into a strong, good-looking man; a real outdoor type.

Six weeks after Lucy's first attempt at gardening, the bed at the front of the house was a riot of colourful flowers: mauves and pinks, deep blues and crimson reds. Jill went up to the attic room so she could look down and make out all the flowery signatures. From her vantage point, she could also see Robert and Lucy laughing and chatting to each other as they pruned the grapevine growing over the front verandah.

The flowers suddenly reminded Jill of the spell that had started this whole planting craze. Now that gardening and Robert filled all her spare time, Lucy seemed to have forgotten all about it. Jill went downstairs and rummaged through the box of books she had pushed under the staircase. As she lifted out the book of spells, the brown wrapping slipped off and a scrap of paper floated down. A line of writing was now visible across the front cover. 'This book belongs to Esther Vizard' Jill read. Vizard. It had been Vizard's Tips, not Wizard's Tips, she realised.

The loose slip of paper looked like it could be the missing section of the love spell. Jill quickly found the torn page. The slip of paper matched exactly. The writing was still faint, but Jill gave a loud laugh as she read the now complete sentence.

'"How to attract lovebirds to your garden".'

She looked out of the front window as Robert and Lucy walked up the path, holding hands. As she watched, Robert leaned down to kiss the top of Lucy's head.

Jill smiled. 'There must have been some magic in that book,' she decided. 'Because that's a pair of lovebirds if ever I saw one.'

Just Desserts

'Oh Libby, listen to this one: "I'm planning to propose to my girlfriend after dinner, please give me all the help you can!" Oh, how sweet. Can I put his hamper together?'

Libby looked across the large kitchen at her cousin. 'Sure. What's he asked for?'

Sasha read the order form, murmuring under her breath. 'He wants an easy-to-heat soup to start, followed by an easy-to-heat casserole and then an easy-to-heat dessert. God, what's with the easy-to-heat business? Does he live in an igloo?'

'No, he probably means something he can microwave.'

'Well, that's not exactly romantic, is it? Imagine, you're in his arms, he's whispering sweet nothings in your ear, the delicious smell of cooking is wafting through the living room, then *ping*, the microwave goes. Dinner is served.'

Libby grinned. 'Sash, we're caterers not cooking police. He

can heat it up with a blow-torch if he wants to.'

'I just think it's a shame. We supply him with the whole package: fantastic food, mood music, coffee-table books as conversation starters,' Sasha waved her arms around the room, pointing at the library of books and CDs, 'even real linen ser-viettes, and he ruins it all with one ping of the microwave.'

Libby was openly laughing at her cousin now. 'Leave that poor man alone. He's obviously so nervous about proposing he can't bear to do the cooking as well. He doesn't need you shouting at him from the sidelines.'

'Well, I just hope his girlfriend knows what she's getting herself into. She might think he's a good cook. What happens when she realises, after she's said yes and it's too late to back out, that he can't cook anything more elaborate than baked beans on toast and he's a big fraud? What does that make us? Accessories after the fact?'

'No, with any luck he'll become completely reliant on us smuggling wonderful meals in to him and become our number-one customer.'

Losing interest in that fax, Sasha picked up the next one on the pile. 'Now, what about this one? "My husband has invited his boss over for dinner and, quite frankly, I couldn't cook my way out of a brown paper bag from McDonald's. Help!!!" You're more like a Good Samaritan than a chef, aren't you, Libby? You should change the name of the company, I reckon. From Big Night In to Big Rescue. But then you'd get all sorts of calls from people – cats stuck up trees, kids down drainpipes, wouldn't you? And you'd have to explain that it's actually a catering company, not an emergency rescue outfit.'

Libby stared at her cousin. Sasha really needed to cut back on the coffee.

'That's right, Sash,' she said carefully. 'Now, how about we start putting the orders together? Can you choose the books and the CDs while I do the shopping lists?'

That worked. For the next fifteen minutes Sasha stood in front of the wall-to-wall library, trying to select coffee-table books and CDs to suit each order.

Revelling in the quiet, Libby looked down once again at the food orders in front of her.

She was catering for six formal dinners, one children's party and one Sunday brunch, all for delivery by six o'clock Saturday evening. She cast a quick eye over the dishes her customers had chosen. Nothing too outlandish or out of the ordinary, she was relieved to see. Most people had stuck to the suggested menus she'd supplied, with just one or two exceptions. Gooseberry fool? She wasn't sure if she'd be able to do that one.

Sasha's voice floated over. 'Libby, what does romantic music mean, exactly? It depends on your taste really, doesn't it? Teenagers would find the Pussycat Dolls romantic, wouldn't they, but they would scare the willies out of an oldie. And I can't imagine a couple of eighteen-years-olds smooching away to Val Doonican or Nana Mouskouri. Should I ring this bloke and ask him to be a bit more specific, do you think?'

'No!' Libby nearly shouted. It was a good thing her cousin

was such a sensational pastrycook, she thought, or she would worry she'd lost all reason hiring her in the first place. 'No, we'll take a punt. What age is he?'

Sasha looked at the form again. 'Oh, he's ancient. Over fifty. Euch! And he's trying to be all romantic. Isn't that the most disgusting thought? Two old people —'

'Sasha! What should he be doing? Ironing his lawn bowls outfit and watching black-and-white movies?' And fifty isn't so old, Libby didn't say out loud. She was only fifteen years off it herself. Oh my God, she thought, realising how true that was.

Sasha laughed. 'Sorry, I'm terrible, aren't I? Just as well you're here to curb my excesses. So let me think. Romantic music. How about a bit of Bach? And then a bit of Burt Bacharach. Bach and Bacharach, geddit? As a kind of theme? Bach-ground for a Bach-analian feast.'

'Sasha, isn't it time you went to the market?'

Sasha looked at her watch.

'It's a bit early, isn't it?'

'No. Goodbye.'

After Sasha had gone, Libby took a moment to relax and have a cup of coffee. She picked up the order form from the man who wanted to propose to his girlfriend. How sweet. And how heartening. Romance was alive and well for a lucky fifty-year-old.

Maybe there was hope for this single 35-year-old yet, she thought.

*

Libby came in early the next day. Friday was Big Night In's most frantic day. There were usually a couple of last-minute orders waiting on the fax machine, despite the plea on their promotional brochure that Thursday was the deadline.

Sure enough, there were two faxes waiting. She'd read through them before Sasha had the chance to grab them and give her running commentary.

The first one was easy – an order for everything needed for a barbecue. *Can you please send us fish, chicken, sausages and lots of salads – don't need the books or the CDs, thanks!* Great. She liked that sort of order.

Libby picked up the second fax. Her heart nearly stopped.

It was from Hayley Kemp.

Hayley Kemp. She couldn't believe it. Hayley Kemp was daring to order a meal from her.

She read it quickly. It was definitely the same Hayley Kemp she used to know. Libby recognised her distinctive flamboyant handwriting. She was surprised Hayley had managed to fill out the order herself. Didn't she have slaves to do this sort of thing these days?

It was a very specific order. Hayley wanted the most up-to-date and innovative Australian cuisine possible. Asian fusion. Bush tucker. All and everything. She wanted two different entrées. Three different main courses. Four – four! – desserts. The latest CDs, all by Australian artists. The latest books, all from Australian authors. There was even a long list of the newspapers and magazines she would like Big Night In to supply.

Libby couldn't believe her eyes. What did Hayley Kemp think she was? A caterer or a set decorator?

She heard the door open behind her. It was Sasha.

'Hi there, Lib. More orders? Gee, people can be thoughtless, can't they? Don't they realise we can't just magic their orders out of nowhere? Anything too complicated?'

Libby just handed her Hayley Kemp's order.

Sasha looked down and gave a low whistle. 'Hayley Kemp? *The* Hayley Kemp?'

Libby nodded. The Hayley Kemp indeed. Socialite. Author. Snob. Idea-snatcher. Client-snatcher. Boyfriend-snatcher.

Yes, that Hayley Kemp.

'You used to work with her, didn't you?' Sasha asked. 'Up in Sydney? Wasn't she that old cow who nicked all your ideas?'

That was putting it mildly, Libby thought. 'Yes, Sasha, *that* old cow. That old schemer. You know the whole story?'

Sasha shook her head. 'Only bits of it. Come on, spill the beans.' She sat down opposite Libby and waited, bright-eyed. She loved a good gossip.

Libby sat down too. 'Hayley and I met at catering school, twelve years ago. We went into business together, running a corporate catering company. It went fine for the first year. Until I realised she was stealing all my ideas and passing them off as her own to private clients she was working for, outside our company. And then she went further – she started contacting our clients on the sly and undercutting our prices, offering to do it on her own, more cheaply. Turned out she'd

been planning to open her own company, using all my con-
tacts and recipes.'

Sasha was wide-eyed. 'How dare she!'

'How dare she is right. She was quite ruthless about it.
And then I discovered she wanted my boyfriend as part of the
package too.'

'That's *awful*,' Sasha breathed. 'She took your clients *and*
your boyfriend?'

Libby nodded. She should have guessed much earlier than
she did. All the flirting. On both sides. But it had been an
awful shock to come home to the flat one night after catering
for a corporate function and find her boyfriend in bed already.
With Hayley.

'And that's why you haven't had a boyfriend since? You've
never got over him?'

Libby was a little stung. 'I have had the occasional boyfriend,
Sasha. You make it sound like I've been living in purdah for
ten years. No, actually, I did get over him. That night, in fact.
I got over a lot that night.'

Libby had dissolved the company there and then. In her
bedroom. She'd practically thrown her boyfriend and Hayley out of the house. She'd considered legal action to get her
clients back and copyright action to get her recipes credited.
Then she'd realised that neither action was worth the bother.
The legal fees would bankrupt her.

So she'd decided to just cut her losses and start over.

She'd moved to Melbourne and started up her own business

again. Hundreds of kilometres from Ms Sneaky Trousers Kemp. But now Ms Sneaky Trousers had come visiting.

Sasha was reading through her order. 'Wow, she's really got a big evening planned, hasn't she? And look at the address.'

Libby glanced over her shoulder. Oh, please don't say Hayley had moved to Melbourne. Please let her just be visiting. This city wasn't big enough for the two of them. No city was big enough for Hayley Kemp.

Sasha whistled. 'The Riverview Hotel Apartments. They're the sensational ones right in the city centre. With all the penthouses. I saw a full-page ad in the paper on the weekend. They've only just opened.'

That would be Hayley, Libby thought. Staying in the trendiest spot in town before anyone else. She wondered who she'd conned to get into there. She was probably staying in the show apartment. It wouldn't be the first time she'd done that.

Hayley was obviously trying to impress someone. Who? Libby wondered.

Hayley had written a mobile number on the fax. Libby couldn't help herself. 'Sasha, can you do me a favour? Ring that number and say you're just looking for some more details about her order. Find out as much as you can, will you? I can't do it, she'll recognise my voice.'

Sasha leapt at the idea. She picked up the phone, cleared her throat and dialled the number.

'Ms Kemp? Good morning. Sasha Delahunty here, from

Big Night In caterers. Thank you so much for your order, it is clear you appreciate quality and excellence.'

Libby had to stop herself laughing. Sasha sounded like she'd spent the past twenty years at a Swiss finishing school.

'No, no, there's no problem at all with your order. It will be our utmost pleasure to meet your every need. But perhaps you can just give me a little more detail about the evening, so we can be sure we have the complete picture and can fulfil your every request.'

Sasha wandered over to the other side of the room. Libby could hear snatches of the conversation.

'Mmm. Yes. Is that right? What a marvellous compliment. Oh yes, indeed, I can think of no finer ambassador for our country's cuisine than you. Yes, of course. By six o'clock. Yes, of course. Thank you, Ms Kemp. Yes, goodbye now.'

She hung up and spun around, grinning at Libby. 'Gee, what a blabbermouth. It's all for an interview she's doing. For a big colour feature in some international magazine. *Foresee* or something, have you heard of it?'

Libby nodded. Of course she'd heard of 4C magazine. She even bought it occasionally. It was the trendsetter's bible, its articles highlighting ideas and fashions months – or some-times years – in advance. How in God's name had Hayley Kemp managed to pull off an interview with that magazine? And why was she doing it in Melbourne? she asked aloud.

Sasha shrugged. 'She said something about Sydney being so yesterday. Everyone's sick of it since the Olympics, she said.

So she's doing the interview here. She said that Melbourne is the new Sydney.'

'Melbourne is the new Sydney? So where does that leave the old Sydney? The real Sydney?'

Sasha shrugged again. 'Dunno. So, anyway, they're doing a feature on her. Dinner with Hayley Kemp. "Food for the new century" or some such thing, she said.'

Libby felt her blood begin to simmer. Then boil. Sasha watched, quite amazed, as mild-mannered Libby blew her top.

'No way, Sasha! Absolutely no way! She did it to me ten years ago; she's not doing it again. Nicking my ideas. Passing them off as her own. To hell with her order. I won't do it.'

Sasha looked a little uncomfortable. 'Um, actually, Libby, she didn't mention you. At all. She probably doesn't even realise it's your company.'

That stopped Libby in her tracks. 'She didn't mention me? At all? Really?'

'No, she just said she'd heard Big Night In was the most innovative of Melbourne's caterers.'

'Did she?'

'She also said money was no object. And she was happy to pay in full in advance if necessary.'

'By cheque?' Libby didn't trust her. That woman had bounced more cheques than Libby had made hot dinners.

'She didn't say.' Sasha was watching her very closely. 'But we can insist on cash. Was she that bad, Lib?'

'She was that bad.'

Sasha beamed. 'So. Have your revenge. Give her an awful meal. Show her up in front of this journalist.'

Libby gave a slow smile. She was tempted. What could Hayley do? If she was going to attempt to pass it off as her own cooking, there'd be no one she could blame, either . . .

She thought about it. She was more than tempted. She was really tempted. Sasha was watching her, all eager-eyed, ready to burst into action.

Then Libby came to her senses and shook her head. It was nearly ten years ago. She'd put it all behind her, surely. She had a very successful business now. It was time she got over Hayley.

'No, Sasha, I don't think so. We won't do anything.' She was glad to hear herself sound like the grown-up voice of reason. 'That's the thing about running a business. You have to learn how to keep your personal feelings separate. Be professional.'

'Oh, Libby, come on. It'd be funny.'

'No, Sasha, I can't do it.'

'Even though she was such a bitch to you in Sydney?'

'Even so.'

'That's your final word?'

'That's my final word.'

'Rats,' Sasha said.

*

By five o'clock on Saturday, the Big Night In kitchen was an absolute hive of activity.

Libby and Sasha had been joined by Alan, the other apprentice chef. The hampers were laid out in long rows. The food was being assembled on the stainless-steel counters, all in the distinctive Big Night In foil containers.

Sasha had just finished putting the last of the CDs, books and magazines into one of the hampers.

'Are you sure the barbecue people didn't want any CDs, Libby?' she called across to her cousin. 'I could put in Cheap Trick's "The Flame", or "Burn for You" by INXS.'

Alan joined in. 'Or what's that old song by Paul Young? You know, that ballad?' He burst into song. '"Every time you go away, you take a piece of meat with you".'

'It's "piece of me", not meat,' Sasha said, snorting with laughter.

Libby grinned. 'Thanks, Sasha, thanks, Alan, that'll be fine. Are we all done? Can I ring the courier?'

They both nodded. The hampers were all lined up, ready to go.

Libby dialled the number. 'Tim? Ready when you are. Two loads tonight, okay? See you soon.'

A little while later, Sasha and Libby sat down to enjoy a glass of wine. Alan had gone home for the night, after helping them to load the first lot of hampers into the back of Tim's van.

'You sure you're okay to help Tim with the other four?' he'd checked with Libby before he left. 'It's a filthy night, with that wind and rain.'

Libby had waved him away. 'No worries, Alan. See you next week.'

Libby had just taken a sip of wine when her mobile rang. 'Big Night In, good evening.'

She listened for a few minutes. 'Oh, Tim, that's awful. Are you okay? The van's okay? And the hampers? You'd already delivered them? No, of course you can't. No, don't worry. Sasha and I are here. We can do them ourselves. Really. Go home, Tim. And don't worry, really.'

She finished the call and turned to Sasha. 'Tim's had an accident. He says the roads are really slippery and the wind has brought some trees down. He didn't see them till it was too late. Nothing serious, but his van's off the road. There's no time to organise another courier. We'll have to deliver the last four hampers ourselves. Do you mind?'

Sasha shook her head. 'No, I'm not going out till nine anyway. Which ones will I do?'

Libby checked the addresses. One in South Melbourne. One in West Melbourne. And two in the inner city.

Including the one to Hayley Kemp.

Well, there was no way she was going to deliver that one herself.

'Will you do Hayley, Sasha? And the other inner-city one? Do you mind?'

'Mind? I'd love to. I can slip a little broken glass into her soup at the last minute. A couple of lizards into her salad. She wanted authentic Australian cuisine, didn't she? And you won't mind, will you?'

Libby wasn't sure if her cousin was joking. 'Sasha,' she warned, 'you won't, will you? Promise me?'

Sasha laughed. 'Of course I won't touch her food. I promise. Cross my heart.'

Libby checked her watch. She'd have to get going to make her deliveries to the other suburbs in time.

'Can you lock up, Sasha, and manage those two hampers?'

'Trust me, dear cousin. Trust me. What is friendship without trust?'

Libby rolled her eyes. Friendship without trust. That was a summary of her friendship with Hayley Kemp, actually. She ruffled her cousin's hair. 'Thanks, Sash. See you Monday.'

Not long after Libby had driven off, Sasha turned off the lights and locked the front door.

She had just climbed into her car and was about to start the engine when she remembered she'd left her street directory in the boot with her two hampers.

She jumped out and opened the hatch. A gust of wind swept in, nearly tearing the door off its hinges. Two pieces of paper started flapping around. Sasha caught them just in time. And just as well, she thought. The delivery addresses were written on them. She secured them back onto the hampers and shut the hatch again.

As she got back into the car and started the engine, she looked back at the hampers. She had put the right addresses on the right hampers, hadn't she?

After all, she wouldn't want to make a mistake, would she? Like accidentally deliver Hayley Kemp's hamper to the other address. And the other hamper to Hayley Kemp . . . Not when their contents were so drastically different.

That would never do, would it? she thought, a smile starting to form. She would hate to ruin Hayley Kemp's night. Ms Hayley Old Cow Kemp. Who had been so mean to her lovely cousin Libby all those years ago. Who was so obviously still trying to pass off Libby's ideas as her own.

Sasha stopped the car suddenly. She couldn't think and drive at the same time.

She had promised Libby, hand on heart, that she wouldn't touch the food in the hampers. But she hadn't promised she wouldn't make a simple mistake and deliver the hampers to the wrong addresses, now, had she?

She looked at her watch. Made her decision. Grinned and started the car.

She'd have to drive fast or she'd be late.

Good. She *loved* driving fast.

*

On the other side of Melbourne, Libby had just delivered the second of her hampers.

She was still smiling from the conversation. The fifty-year-old man was a true romantic. His house had looked lovely, the fire flickering in the grate, candles lit. It looked so cosy, especially with the wild weather howling outside.

Libby couldn't wait to get home. She was always exhausted by Saturday night. The last thing she felt like was going out. She'd go home to her little flat, heat up a casserole, open a bottle of wine, light the fire and have a nice, long soak in the bath . . .

Her mobile phone rang. Uh oh, she thought. Sasha.

It wasn't Sasha, though.

It was a male voice. But the line was so bad it kept breaking up. Oh hell, Libby thought, remembering that she hadn't charged her mobile that morning. They'd been so busy she'd forgotten. She checked the battery. It was right down.

She pulled over. Maybe that would help. She could get this call at least. And then recharge the battery as soon as she got home. 'I'm very sorry, could you say all that again?'

The voice crackled, breaking up now and again. 'Is th— Big Ni— In? The caterers?'

'Yes,' Libby shouted. 'Libby Smith speaking.'

'Hello, Lib—, this is Ned Ra—. I'm lookin— aft—er my — bir—day par—y. Ord—ed the foo— you. —t of a prob— can you — '

Libby felt like shaking the mobile. She'd only got a bit of

that. But had she heard the word problem? She didn't like that word. Not on her work mobile.

'There's a problem with your order, did you say? Ned, is it? What kind of problem?'

'I —n't qu— know what to —'

This was no good, Libby thought. 'Where are you?'

He had to repeat his address three times before she got it.

'I'm not far from you. I'll be there soon,' she shouted.

Fifteen minutes later Libby pulled up in front of a small terrace house. There was a bedraggled bunch of balloons tied to the gate, being buffeted by the gusty wind. She clambered out and ran up the path, ducking her head against the rain and knocked at the door.

An agitated orange-haired clown answered.

'Ned?' she said, trying not to laugh.

'Libby? From the caterers?'

She nodded.

He smiled a big clowny smile. 'Thank you so much for coming by. I'm sorry to sound so stupid, I'm actually just supposed to be helping my sister out. But she works in the emergency services and got called away to help with the storms. So I've been left in charge and, quite frankly, I'm baffled.'

It was a little bit hard to take a man in a frizzy orange wig seriously. She had to ask. 'And your clothes? Are you normally dressed like this?'

He laughed then. 'Believe me, this is the first time. And the last too. My sister asked me when I was jetlagged last week and I was in no sound mind to say no. It's her daughter's birthday party.'

Libby followed him inside as they spoke. 'Jetlagged? Where had you flown from?'

'Canada,' he said. 'I've been working over there for the past four years. Just came home last week.'

She nodded. She thought he had a touch of an accent. 'Well, lead me to the kids. And the hamper. What exactly is the problem?'

He looked very embarrassed again. 'I hope you don't think I'm too thick. Debbie, my sister, said she'd ordered a whole lot of kids' food from you. But I'm just not sure how to serve it.'

Libby remembered the order now. It was standard kids' party food. No tricks to serving it. Poor man must still be jetlagged.

Libby walked into the living room. It was like walking into a fairy glen. Eight little girls, all dressed as fairies, were waving their wands and doing trit-trotty dances across the floor.

Music was blaring out of the CD player. Libby winced. It was some sort of modern jazz. All squealing trumpets and snare drums. Very modern kids in this house, by the sound of things.

Libby followed Ned into the kitchen. The hamper Sasha had delivered was on the counter, with a long row of little foil containers lined up beside it.

'It won't take me a moment to sort all this out,' Libby said cheerily. 'Those kids must be getting very hungry.'

'They're like wild animals,' Ned admitted. 'Hyenas. Ready to tear me limb from limb with hunger. It's more like *Dances with Wolves* in there than *Swan Lake*.'

She grinned at him. He was really very sweet. She wondered what he looked like without all that face make-up. And that orange wig. And dressed in something other than a baggy orange all-in-one suit.

'Well, don't worry, I'll have them fed in just a moment.' Libby opened the first container and her stomach gave a flip. She opened the second. Then the third. And the fourth. Faster and faster, until they were all open.

She looked down at them. Then looked up at Ned.

He smiled again, the effect spoilt a little by the mad make-up. 'I'm happy to help serve it to them. I'm just not sure where to start.'

Libby swallowed. She could tell him where to start. It was quite easy. You started with the sushi and sashimi. Followed by the emu pâté. Then the wattleseed pasta. Then the other six dishes which perfectly demonstrated innovative Australian cuisine.

It was obvious what had happened. Sasha had dropped off the wrong hamper. Which meant that she had dropped off the wrong hamper to the other address too.

Which meant that around about now, just a few kilometres away, Hayley Kemp was probably opening her hamper. Opening her little foil containers. And preparing to serve the influential *4C* magazine journalist a fine dinner of Vegemite sandwiches. Mashed potato and sausages. Aeroplane jelly and lolly snakes.

Washed down with hot, milky Milo.

With the *Best of the Wiggles* CD playing in the background.

Libby looked at her watch. There was still time. She could pack this up again. Drive across town. Switch the hampers. Make sure Hayley Kemp's evening wasn't ruined after all. Or . . .

She could turn down the volume on her mobile.

Switch it off, even. Because she'd bet a million dollars it was just about to ring.

She could reassure Ned that everything was just fine. That this was standard Australian children's party fare these days. Tell him a lot had changed while he'd been in Canada.

She looked at him. He looked back at her. She noticed what lovely eyes he had. The blue clown make-up seemed to accentuate the colour.

There was a sudden chant from the living room. 'We want food! We want food! We want food!'

Ned looked really worried. Scared, almost. He touched her arm briefly. 'Libby, if you stay, I owe you. For ever. Lunch, dinner, whatever you like.'

That clinched it.

'Of course I'll stay. And don't worry, this food looks much scarier than it is. It won't take me a minute to show the girls how to use chopsticks. Or eat the pâté. If we need to, we'll tell them it's magical fairy food from a land far, far away . . .'

He smiled in relief. 'Thanks, Libby.'

She smiled back. 'It's my pleasure, really.' She reached into her handbag and turned off her mobile phone. 'Now then, where would we find the plates?'

One hour later, the little girls were having sword fights with the chopsticks Libby had found in the bottom of a kitchen cupboard.

But Libby and Ned hardly noticed them. They were too busy talking, eating and laughing.

Four months later, Libby and Ned were curled up on her sofa, reading the Sunday newspapers and finishing their Thai takeaway.

The afternoon sunshine spilled into their flat. A light breeze ruffled the curtains at the open window behind them.

'More wine, sweetheart?' Ned said.

Libby looked up. 'Oh, great, thanks, Ned.' She held up her glass and smiled at him as he poured the wine. She loved their Sunday lunches. Long, leisurely afternoons that usually stretched into long, leisurely nights together.

He grinned at her. His smile still made her heart skip. And his eyes had turned out to be even nicer without the clown make-up. Who'd have thought such a treasure was lurking under that bright-orange wig and costume that night?

Ned refilled his own glass, then went back to the newspaper. The room was quiet for a moment.

Then he laughed out loud. 'People really are unbelievable. Listen to this, Lib: "A respected trend-forecasting magazine has predicted a return to childhood food as the next big thing in cuisine, with an Australian food expert playing a major role in the resurgence."'

Libby looked up. Childhood food? Australian food expert? Ned read on.

'"In the new issue of *4C* magazine, Sydney-based food queen Hayley Kemp explains the new theory. 'As the world gets faster and more impersonal I believe we will all be looking for safety and a return to the innocence of childhood. It isn't so much a fashion statement as a return to traditional values, in food as well as behaviour.'"'

Libby shut her eyes.

Ned looked at her and smiled. 'Come on now, Lib. Pay attention, your customers will be queuing up for this soon.' He started reading aloud again. '"If Hayley and her fellow futurists have their way, dinner parties of the future will feature simple fare like Vegemite sandwiches, sausages and mashed potato, hot milky Milo to drink and for dessert . . ."'

Libby interrupted. 'Don't tell me, Ned. Jelly and lolly snakes?'

He looked up in surprise. Libby was now lying stretched out on the sofa, the cushion over her face. She seemed to be groaning. Or laughing. He couldn't tell which. 'Yes, jelly and lolly snakes for dessert . . . Sorry, Libby, have you read this already?'

She looked up at him, shook her head and smiled. 'No. No, I haven't.'

'Then I'm even more impressed with you. You really do have your finger on the catering pulse, don't you?'

She stood up suddenly, came over to him and planted a big kiss right on his lips.

'Yes, I do, don't I?'

Then she took the newspaper out of his hand and threw it out the window.

Sweet Charity

Lola Quinlan leaned over the counter and took the bundle of second-hand clothes from the grey-haired woman. 'Margaret, you are not just one of my dearest friends but one of my best suppliers. Thank you so much.'

'They're seriously back-of-the-wardrobe outfits, Lola. Nothing too flash at all, I'm afraid.'

'Someone will love them, I'm sure. I'm delighted you came in. I've put aside a new outfit just for you.'

'Oh, Lola, no. I can't buy anything else. I've just done a big clear-out at home.'

'But you can't leave a charity shop empty-handed. Or charities shop, as I should call it. Do you know, last year alone we helped fund a new playground, bought the equivalent of two tyres for a runabout bus for the old ones in the nursing home and sent two poor families away on breaks. All from a small shop filled with second-hand clothes and bric-a-brac. Imagine. So it's not so much about buying a new outfit, Margaret, as being a part of the community.'

Margaret shook her head, laughing. 'You just won't take no for an answer, will you?'

'Not if I can help it,' Lola said, smiling. 'Now, let me fetch this suit for you. You always look so stylish in darker colours and I think this one will be right up your street.'

Margaret waited while Lola went through the floral curtain into the stockroom. Her friend really did have a good eye for other people's style. It was just her own clothing that would nearly take the eye out of you. Tartan with paisley prints. Culottes with vests. Sometimes as many as six strands of beads. Last year she'd taken to wearing flowers pinned to her outfits, often with a matching one in her hair. It was her Rio look, she'd told Margaret.

Lola emerged carrying a beautifully made tailored jacket with a matching mid-length skirt. 'What do you think, Margaret? I thought of you as soon as I saw it.'

'That's because it's my suit. I donated it to you last week. Don't you remember?'

'Oh, so you did. Well, I think you acted too soon. You'll get a few more wears out of it yet. I'll pop it in a bag for you, will I?'

Two schoolgirls came into the shop just as Margaret left. She'd not only taken the suit back home but also paid ten dollars for it.

'Hello, girls. Can I help you?' Lola's Irish accent rang clear across the room.

'No, we're right, thanks.'

'Are you looking for anything in particular?'

The taller one spoke. 'Um, actually, we're having a fancy dress theme for the end-of-school-year disco and we're looking for something.'

'Oh, that would be the bad taste party, would it?'

They looked relieved. 'You know about it?'

Lola stepped out from behind the counter, turning slowly so they could see the paisley kaftan she was wearing. 'I've had three offers for this dress already. Imagine. Wouldn't you think they'd have more sympathy for an elderly lady like myself, getting dressed in the morning, eyesight fading . . .' She stopped and looked at the shorter of the two girls. 'Emily, hello there. I didn't recognise you in your school uniform.'

The girl was now bright red. 'Hello, Lola.'

'Will we be seeing you again this weekend? I heard from my son that you did a marvellous job waitressing at the wedding last week.' Lola and her family owned and ran a motel with function rooms just north of the town. 'It's certainly not the easiest of jobs for a first-timer either, but I know he was very pleased indeed with you.'

Emily nodded enthusiastically. 'I really enjoyed it. Mr Quinlan asked me to come and work this Saturday night too. And maybe Sunday lunchtime if you get enough bookings.'

'Isn't that terrific! I'll pop over to the dining room and

say hello. Now, don't be shy. Have a good poke around. I'm unpacking new things all the time too, so if you don't find anything here today, be sure to come back tomorrow.'

Fifteen minutes later, Lola was alone in the shop again. Two schoolboys had come in after Emily and her friend had left. The boys had rustled half-heartedly through the rack of CDs and old records before wandering out again, all without any eye contact with her. She was used to that. It didn't bother her. Teenage boys were much more fun to watch than talk to, she had discovered. They gave away so much, for all their strut and confidence and swagger. Bags of nerves and hormones.

She had learned more about people by working in a charity shop than in all the years of running motels and guesthouses. She had never been snobbish about selling – or buying – second-hand goods. In fact, when she moved from Ireland to Australia as a twenty-year-old, nearly sixty years ago now, charity shops had been her lifeline. Shortly after arriving she had found herself on her own with a small son. She had dressed herself and her son, and in later years her three grand-daughters, too, in second-hand clothing.

She liked to make up a story for each item in the shop. She imagined the goods talking to each other after she had closed up for the night. 'I used to belong to a lady who breeds horses,' a tweed jacket would say. 'Did you? I came out from Italy when my owner emigrated ten years ago,' a CD of opera songs would answer. 'I'm from overseas too,' a French scarf would pipe up from the scarf rack.

Lola had just finished polishing the wooden counter-top when the door opened. A rush of hot air came in with the new arrival. Late November in South Australia was like living in an oven, Lola thought. The heat still astounded her.

She smiled a welcome at the woman, assessing her quickly. Fifty-ish. A faded, soft prettiness but some sadness in the face. A weariness. Lola didn't know her. She was either a new arrival to the area or a visitor. People often dropped their clothes in to charity shops far from their own homes. 'Good afternoon. Can I help you?'

'Good afternoon.' The woman hesitated, then moved closer. 'I was wanting to donate some clothes if I could.'

'How kind of you. We're always grateful to receive whatever people can give.' She waited. The woman was carrying a suit bag but seemed reluctant to pass it over. 'Would you like me to take that?'

'Oh. Yes. Thank you.' She still didn't move.

Lola looked closer. The woman was more than tired. Her eyes were strained. Red-rimmed too. Lola made a show of looking at her watch. 'I was just about to make myself a cup of tea. Nothing more cooling in this hot weather. Could I make you one while I'm there? I'm sure you don't want to be going out in that heat again yet.'

'Well, thank you, but . . . are you sure?'

'Couldn't be surer. I'm Lola Quinlan, by the way.'

'Oh. Hello, Lola. I'm Patricia. Patricia Nolan.'

Lola moved a chair to the side of the counter, out of sight of any passers-by. 'Now, you settle yourself there for a moment and I'll be right back.'

She prepared the tray quickly. Not for her grubby coffee mugs and tea bags. In her first week as a volunteer at the charity shop she had brought in a nice set of china tea cups and saucers, a proper kettle and an even nicer tea pot. 'Irish Breakfast tea, I thought,' she called over. 'I know it's much later than breakfast, but it's such a reviving flavour, I find.'

'That would be lovely, thank you.'

Lola added a little jug of milk, slices of lemon, sugar cubes and the dainty biscuits Katie from the bakers across the road had dropped in that morning. She placed the tray gently on the counter, then moved to the door and turned the sign so it read *Back shortly*.

Patricia looked concerned. 'Oh, you don't have to close on my account.'

'It's union rules. A little break now and again and I find I'm much more inclined to do the hard selling when I'm called upon.'

'Is that an Irish accent?'

'It is indeed. Though I'm practically Australian these days. Three-quarters of my life spent here just about qualifies me, don't you think?'

Patricia nodded. 'My husband was Irish too. Well, his parents were. He loved it. We went there once, and he said it was like finding his spiritual home. He'd talk to anyone at the drop of a hat, you see, so we hardly had to go into a pub together and —'

Lola had seen it coming. As Patricia started to cry, she reached over and took the cup from her hand. Patricia lifted both hands to her face and sobbed. The suit bag stayed on her lap. She still hadn't passed it over.

'Did those suits belong to your husband?' Lola asked gently.

A nod. 'He —' She stopped, her voice breaking.

Lola waited, wondering. Had the man died, or left her, or . . .

'He had a heart attack.' The words came falteringly at first, and then in a rush. 'There was no chance, no warning even. We were packing to go on holiday, and he had just laid all these suits out on the bed and we were laughing, saying it was women who were supposed to be the world's worst packers, but it always took him longer. I'd gone out to the line to bring in his shirts, ready to go in the case. And when I came in, he was —'

Lola stayed silent, reaching for the box of tissues on the counter beside her and passing it to the other woman.

After a while Patricia spoke again. 'I didn't know what to do. I knew I should have rung someone, but the phone was in the kitchen and it would have meant leaving him and I couldn't . . . he was in my arms.' The tears came again. 'I knew he was already dead, and then about an hour later, our son came home, he was supposed to be driving us to the airport, and he came in and —'

This time Lola moved. She held the woman as she sobbed

into her shoulder. 'I'm so sorry for you. It must have been a very hard time.'

Patricia was embarrassed, wiping her eyes with a tissue. 'I'm so sorry. I don't know where that came from.' She gave a little, sad laugh. 'I mean, I do, but I thought I was getting better. It's just between the moving and packing up and . . .' The whole story came out. Patricia and her son had moved to the Clare Valley two weeks previously. He was starting an apprenticeship in the new year and Patricia had a part-time job as a secretary at the hospital.

'I thought a fresh start would be the best thing. That if I wasn't in the house we had lived in together, the memories wouldn't hit me every day. I meant to give all his clothes away last year, but I couldn't. I brought them all with me. And when I was unpacking yesterday, I thought, this is ridiculous, he's not coming back. Luke doesn't want to wear them. He finds it just as hard as I do. But it took me all day to put them into the suit bag and I walked past here three times as it was.'

'Would you like me to take a look at them? Only if you want to. Or you can take them back home if you'd prefer.' As Patricia glanced towards the door, Lola continued. 'It's nearly five. I'd say we'll be on our own from now on, anyway.'

Patricia's hands were shaking as she undid the zip. 'He loved suits. He was always really well dressed. That was the first thing I noticed about him when we met.' She started to take three of them out at once, when Lola stopped her.

'Oh, Patricia, you're going much too fast for me. I'm an

elderly woman even though I'm sure you think I'm only in my mid-forties. Why don't you take them out one at a time and tell me a little bit about them? Now, that jacket there in the front. Are my eyes deceiving me or is that Donegal tweed?'

'Yes. Yes, it is.'

Lola nodded, pleased. 'The finest in all Ireland, I always thought. Tell me, did your husband – what was his name?'

'Brendan.'

'Did Brendan choose that one himself or did you have a hand in it? And where were you when you bought it? All the details, now, mind. If there's one thing I love it's hearing the stories behind clothes.'

'We were on holidays in Ireland. Actually, it was our wedding anniversary. Brendan's idea. He had surprised me. I thought we were going to Sydney, so I wasn't surprised when we went to the airport. He and Luke had planned it all. We drove to the international airport. Brendan was like that, just loved surprises. And somehow we got upgraded into business class. He kept looking over and saying, "I told you to stick with me, Pat. Didn't I promise you a life of luxury?"'

'Oh, a man with style. I like the sound of him already. Go on . . .'

Two days later, Lola was unfolding a new delivery of shirts when the door opened. She looked up and smiled a welcome as a young man made his way to the counter.

'Hello, Lola? I'm Luke, my mum said —'

'Of course. Patricia's son? Hello, Luke. It's a pleasure to meet you.' A nice-looking lad. Thick brown hair. Soft eyes. Sad eyes too, she thought. A lot for a teenage lad, his father dying, moving house, starting a new job . . .

'Mum said you would be interested in taking some of our old books? I have them in the car.'

She peered out of the window. A bright-orange Torana that looked like it had seen better, more fashionable days was parked outside. 'That's yours?'

He nodded.

'You certainly wouldn't get lost in a snowstorm in that little number.'

He grinned. 'I'm saving for a Porsche.'

'I don't know. That's more distinctive in its own way.'

He started carrying the books in. There were four small boxes, all full.

'Thank you, Luke. We always need new stock.'

He hesitated. 'Mum said you were really kind to her the other afternoon. Thanks.'

He was looking awkward, but she admired his manners and his courage. 'Please tell your mum she's welcome to pop in any time she likes. I'd love to have another chat.'

'She misses Dad so much. And I've tried to help but . . .' His voice trailed off.

'You've probably helped her more than you know.'

He shrugged and she saw that mixture of vulnerability and

bravado again. Time for a change of subject, she decided. 'Luke, I wonder if you could give me some advice? Those CDs and records there have just arrived, but I'm afraid I haven't a clue about them. I really can't tell one modern band from another. I don't suppose you'd be interested in sorting through them for me? I can't pay you for the work, but I can promise you one free CD an hour.' He didn't need to know she'd put the money in the till for them herself.

'Oh, cool. Sure, that'd be great. I have to do some stuff for Mum, but I could come back later?'

'Perfect. See you then.'

She and Luke spent a pleasant hour or two together, chatting sometimes, working quietly together other times. After four o'clock their solitude was interrupted as waves of school-kids started coming in. She made a point of welcoming each of them. A tip she'd read in an anti-shoplifting pamphlet. Mind you, if people were shoplifting from a charity shop, they were either in dire straits or particularly shameless.

She caught the eye of one girl. 'You're looking for something for the bad taste party?'

Up came the colour as she nodded. Beside her, her two friends were now also looking embarrassed. Teenagers really were so sweet, Lola thought. She pointed to the rack behind them.

'I've put a few things to one side for that very event. Mind you, my idea of bad taste and yours might be something quite different.' She knew they were looking at her outfit. A green trouser suit today, with a yellow polka-dot shirt underneath. She'd teamed it with a bandanna, jauntily tied in a bow on one side. 'So before you ask, no, I'm afraid this isn't for sale.'

Fifteen minutes later they left, each with an outfit for the party. Three young men came in next. Lola smiled a welcome, called out a hello, but they ignored her, talking among themselves.

Flick, flick. The tallest of them picked his way along the rail, sending the clothes hangers rattling. 'We should just raid my dad's wardrobe for this thing. You should see the shit he wears.'

Lola winced. 'Excuse me?'

'His suits are crap. And he's got this golfing gear he wears every weekend. Jesus Christ, he looks like some fat man from the seventies.'

'Excuse me?'

That time he heard her. He turned. 'What?'

'I'd prefer it if you didn't swear like that while you are in this shop.'

He gave a dismissive laugh. 'You'd what?'

Lola kept her voice calm. 'Could you please mind your language while you are in here?'

'You've got to be joking.' He laughed, looked at the two others with him and rolled his eyes. One of them nervously giggled. 'It's a crappy charity shop.'

'It's a charity shop, yes.'

She stared him down. He shrugged and turned away.

'Come on. Let's get out of here,' the smaller of the three said.

'No.' It was the one who had sworn. 'I haven't looked around yet.' He pushed back one row of suit jackets, flicked through another rack, then went to the shelf of records and CDs. Luke was there, sorting the final shelf. The boy ignored him.

'Did you hear about Kane and the party?' The smallest one spoke to the other boy. His voice was breaking. Lola could tell by the squeak appearing now and again. 'It's wicked. Go on, tell Jed about your harem, Kane.'

Kane shrugged. 'It's no big deal.'

'Come on. What is it?' said the other boy, Jed.

The smallest boy glanced over at Kane, as if to check it was all right for him to tell the story. Lola was reminded of films featuring a prince or a lord arrogantly striding around, while his acolytes bowed and scraped and did their best to get his attention.

'He's asked four different girls. So each of them thinks he's their date and then they'll all turn up!'

Jed frowned. 'But why?'

Kane reached over and gave him a clip. 'Because it'll be funny. I'm going to pretend I've had concussion, and can't remember inviting any of them. Meanwhile they'll all have had the excitement of being asked out by *moi*.' The other two sniggered at his French accent. Kane turned back to the CDs, flicking through with one finger. 'And Jesus, it's not as if anyone else is lining up to ask them out.'

He returned to the clothes racks and selected a bright-orange shirt and a blue-and-white patterned tie, then strolled over to the counter and tossed them on top. 'I'll take those.'

'No you won't,' Lola said.

'What?'

'I said, no you won't take those. This is a charity shop. So you will pay for them and if you have any manners at all, you'll say please and thank you.'

'Oh, forget it.' Leaving the clothes on the counter, he and his two followers sauntered out.

Little pup, Lola thought. It had been foolish of her to stand up to him. She'd heard enough horror stories of shop assistants being robbed or even attacked, but she just couldn't abide bad manners like that. She looked over at Luke and shook her head. 'I don't know, the young people of today . . .'

'Bring back the whip,' he said with a grin.

On Sunday afternoon Lola called into the motel restaurant just as Emily was finishing setting the last of the tables. She looked with pleasure at the tidy room and the perfectly folded serviettes. 'Oh, that's lovely, Emily. Thank you. You're doing so well.'

A shy smile. 'Thank you.'

'Did you get anything for the bad taste party yet?'

'I've got a few ideas. It's a bit tricky, actually. You want to be bad taste but you also want to look good, you know, so —'

'Of course. Are you going on your own, or do you have a date?'

'I've got a date.'

'How marvellous. Who is he?'

'It's a bit of a secret. Will you promise not to tell anyone?'

'I promise.' Lola had a sinking feeling. The blush was the giveaway.

'It's Kane Gooding.'

'Kane? I don't think I know him,' she pretended, hiding her concern behind a cheery voice. Perhaps there were two Kanes in the school.

Emily was flushed with pleasure now. 'He's tall, with light-brown hair. His dad runs that property company.' She giggled softly. 'He's sort of the school heart-throb. That's what I mean about the bad taste theme being tricky. I want to look bad and look good all at the same time.'

Oh poor little Emily, Lola thought. By the time she real-ised what Kane had done to her, she wouldn't care what she looked like.

Lola was torn between letting Emily enjoy the feeling and telling her the truth behind Kane's invitation. She opened her mouth and then shut it again, quickly. She couldn't inter-fere. Emily wasn't her daughter or granddaughter. She didn't really have any responsibility for her, did she? And sometimes you had to let young people make mistakes, suffer heart-aches, otherwise they would never learn their own way in the world. She'd learnt that raising her son, and then her three granddaughters. Fighting against all her impulses, Lola smiled brightly. 'Well, I hope you have a lovely night.'

Emily blushed again. 'Thanks, Lola. Me too.'

The next day, the small spotty boy returned to the shop on his own. Lola wasn't surprised when he went straight to the rack and picked out the orange shirt and the blue patterned tie. Kane had obviously sent one of his followers in to do his bad taste shopping. How brave.

'How much are these, please?'

'Let me just check. Oh, the label seems to have fallen off. Will you help me find it?'

It had fallen onto the floor. The boy picked it up and handed it across with a smile. 'Here it is.'

'Thank you, my dear,' Lola said. What was a nice boy like him doing mixed up with a bully like Kane Gooding? she wondered. 'While you're here, would you mind just helping me move this rack?'

As they shifted it – she'd be shifting it back just as soon as he was gone – she noticed Kane loitering across the street. 'Your friend is a bit of a hit with the girls, is he?'

The boy shrugged.

'He's collecting a harem, you said. For that party.'

'It's not doing anyone any harm. It makes them feel good, and it'll be a laugh on the night.'

Lola pasted on a smile. 'It sure will be. I know Emily, but who were the others he invited?' She smoothly spoke over his surprise. 'Just in case they come in looking for clothes, I don't want to give the game away. It being such a good joke and all.'

The boy weighed her up for a moment and then seemed to decide she wasn't joking. 'Lisa Richards, Karlie Talbot and that Emily. I don't think he's decided on the fourth one yet.'

'Oh, he's a real scamp, isn't he? Well, I hope you all have a good time.'

She tapped her fountain pen against her chin as she watched the boy deliver the clothes to Kane across the road. A real scamp indeed.

The night of the bad taste party arrived. Lola had decided she needed to be there, to see the fallout and make sure the girls were okay. Especially Emily. She had chatted with her several times at the motel, and liked her more and more each time.

It had taken just a couple of phone calls to organise things for tonight. Lola smiled across the front seat of the car at her new friend. 'Thank you so much for this, Patricia. I do still like to drive, but I found the police don't have the same relaxed attitude about an octogenarian behind the wheel.'

'It's my pleasure, Lola. I'm enjoying myself.'

In the back seat Margaret leaned forward. 'This is like watching one of those wildlife documentaries, isn't it?'

Lola and Patricia laughed. That was exactly what it was like, seeing all the plumed and preened teenagers circling each other, the body language, the awkwardness, the mock confidence. They were parked across the road from the school hall, just close enough to have a full view of the front steps and hear snatches of conversations. As the three of them chattered they watched couple after couple meet up. Nervous boys stood at the door. Out of cars spilled young women in the most extraordinary outfits. Their idea of bad taste was certainly different from hers, Lola decided. She liked some of the outfits. She'd never understood this idea of stripes not going with spots. Quite eye-catching, in her opinion.

'That's him, there,' she hissed suddenly. Kane, in that orange shirt and blue tie. And there was his entourage. They watched as he took up position on the steps. Emily had told her he'd asked her to meet him at exactly eight o'clock. He'd insisted that she not be late. He'd told her that punctuality meant a lot to him. It was only good manners, he'd said. Emily had been very taken with that.

Lola checked her watch. One minute to eight. Then thirty seconds. There was a good crowd around, boys and girls. Kane had obviously arranged to have an audience.

Eight o'clock came. In the middle, Kane's smile was getting wider and wider.

By five past it wasn't quite so wide. There was some shifting of feet. Some awkward glancing at watches.

A voice came from the huddle behind him. 'Looks like you've been stood up, mate!'

Kane spun around. 'Who said that?' No one owned up.

By ten past, most of the group had started filtering into the hall, laughing loudly, wanting to share the news with the rest of the group already inside. There were still about fifteen people waiting outside when the noise of a car caught their attention.

A bright-orange Torana drew up right to the foot of the steps. A 1970s song blared from the car as the doors were flung open. 'Born to be Alive' by Patrick Hernandez.

In one swift choreographed movement, four young women stepped out, slamming the doors firmly behind them. Their hair was teased. Their fishnet and leopard-skin stockings were torn. Their clothes were a ragbag of chiffon, animal print and nylon. It was as if a feral version of the Spice Girls had arrived. With just the smallest of stumbles, they lined up in a row, put their arms around each other and walked, heads held high, straight past Kane, past his friends and into the hall. Emily's head was held highest of all.

'Hey!' It was Kane. They ignored him.

'Stood up not just once, but four times, mate,' Lola said softly.

The orange car pulled away from the steps, turned in a slow semi-circle and then pulled in beside the car Lola and her two friends were sitting in.

Luke wound down his window. 'Hi, Mum. Hi, Lola. Hi, Mrs Hendon.'

'Luke, what excellent driving. Well done,' Lola called across. 'You'll be a rally-car driver yet.'

He grinned. 'So how do you think that went?'

'Like clockwork. The girls looked marvellous.'

'That's one word for it,' Luke said.

Lola had had a wonderful evening at the motel with the four girls, getting them ready. As it turned out she hadn't needed to bring anything from the charity shop. There'd been plenty enough in her own wardrobe. They had tried on different out-fits with great enthusiasm. Patricia had been called in to help with the make-up and had done an appropriately terrible job. Margaret had helped with their hair.

If Lola had had any lingering doubts about telling Emily and the other three the truth about Kane's invitation, they'd been short-lived. As soon as the four girls had arrived at the motel, she knew she'd made the right decision. She'd seen instantly that Kane had picked on four of the most vulnerable girls in the school. Karlie with her stutter, but with such beautiful eyes. Lisa, overweight certainly, but what a bright mind. The fourth girl – the one who had been the hardest for Emily to track down – was Shana. Poor little Shana, with her buck teeth and her sweet nature. And of course there had been Emily, shy, blushing Emily.

Lola had called over to speak to Emily three days earlier, just as she was finishing her waitressing shift. She'd wrestled with her decision for days before she'd finally made up her mind. Yes, there were times when young people had to learn from their own mistakes. But she'd decided this wasn't one of those times.

She went straight to the point. 'Emily, you might think I'm interfering, but I've become privy to some information that might concern you. I don't want you to be hurt, but you might want to check it out, and if it's true, perhaps you would tell me. There might be a way we can fix things.' Then Lola had told her all she'd heard in the charity shop.

Emily did check. It was true. Kane had invited the four of them, in exactly the same way. Sidling up to them at lunchtime. Stressing the importance of punctuality. Swearing them to secrecy. And each had accepted.

By the time Emily reported back, Lola had hatched her plan. Luke was drafted in to drive the girls. It was a way of introducing them to him, and him to them, and, as he said himself, he had the perfect car for a bad taste party.

'Such a shame you couldn't have gone in there with them,' she said to him now.

'Oh, they're not staying. They'll be out in a minute. That's why I'm waiting here.'

'They're not staying?' She hadn't known about this. That was the whole idea, for them to have fun in the party together, in front of everyone and especially in front of Kane and his cronies.

'No. They decided on the way here they only wanted to stay for one song. We all thought it would be much more fun to go out for pizza together instead. That's all right, Mum, isn't it?'

'Of course,' Patricia said.

Lola decided she was even more pleased with the new plan. She pretended not to be. 'You're going to be seen in public with the four of them? In those clothes? What will people think?'

'That you had something to do with it, probably,' Margaret said drily.

'We were actually wondering if the three of you would like to join us,' Luke said.

Lola sounded shocked. 'What? With those four dressed like that? And you, in that car?' She turned to the other two women. 'What do you two think?'

Margaret, sporting one of Lola's chiffon ponchos and silver eyeshadow, nodded enthusiastically. Patricia, resplendent in a purple crimplene kaftan with dangling moon-shaped earrings, did too. After a glass of champagne at the motel, they'd been more than happy to dress up as well.

'What about you, Lola?' Luke asked.

She paused as if giving it some thought, quickly adjusting the draped scarf on her tiger-print pantsuit and slipping her feet back into her gold rope sandals. She wouldn't miss it for the world. It was just a shame she hadn't had time to get dressed up tonight too. Never mind. With luck no one would notice her ordinary outfit among the others. She gave the fake orchid pinned in her hair a final tweak and then beamed across at him.

'I'd be honoured,' she said.

The Long Way Home

Shelley made the age limit for the ten-city *Rave* tour of Europe by two months and three weeks. The woman in the travel agency pointed out that fact as she ran her eyes down the application form.

'You're thirty-four? Nearly thirty-five? Our clients do tend to be the younger end of the age group. You're sure you're happy to go ahead? We've other tours with more of a focus on culture, less on —'

'No, I'm very happy with this one, thanks.' Shelley had her hand on the brochure on the desk between them as if she was staking a claim.

The woman lowered her voice. 'They're usually all single, not really into the history side of things. More out for a good time.'

Shelley dug out a bright smile from somewhere. 'I am too, I

promise.' A pause. Then her confidence faltered. 'Don't I look like I am?'

The other woman seemed relieved when her phone rang.

At home, on the new sofa in the centre of the living room which still felt nothing like home even after three months, Shelley leafed through her ticket folder and read the brochure. All the people in the *Rave* photos looked like models. Happy models. Happy and high-on-life models. She'd have to do her best to look like them. She had obviously not dressed casually enough that morning. She pulled her hair out of its current plait. Made a mental note to buy some T-shirts. Decided to wash her jeans a few unnecessary times to fade them. She automatically went to the towel cupboard to get the washing powder when she realised that was where she'd kept it in her old house. In their old house. In her new house, she kept it under the sink.

She'd seen the *Rave* ad on TV the previous week, rung the toll-free number for the brochure and picked out the tour that lasted two weeks and took in ten European cities, finishing with a visit to Edinburgh and the highlands of Scotland. She read the description, fighting her way through the exclamation marks that surrounded the brief eligibility questionnaire. Yes, she was between eighteen and thirty-five. Yes, she was single. As of three months previously. Yes, she was out for a good time. 'Are you looking for carefree days of fun, adventure and romance? We supply three out of three!' the *Rave* copywriter promised.

Travel was the key, Shelley had heard. Lose yourself and

find yourself at the same time. She had a different motto in mind. Run, run, run as fast as you can. She couldn't get away from her own life fast enough.

Her taxi was delayed the morning the tour group left. She heard the driver make his excuses about heavy traffic and oil spills but she was too nervous to console him the way she normally would. She needed him to concentrate on his driving and get her there before she changed her mind. She was the last to arrive at the meeting point in the departure area. She knew immediately it was a mistake. She should have got there first. She could have welcomed the others, been someone they came to and wanted to talk to, instead of having to edge in and join the group, feeling left out on the sidelines. She hated being late. She was always the first to arrive anywhere. Harry said it was from being the daughter of a schoolteacher.

They'd been late for the first appointment at the maternity hospital. She'd been fidgeting in her seat, willing the tram to go faster. He'd taken her hand and squeezed it.

'Shell, relax. We're about a minute late, that's all.'

'What if they give our appointment to someone else?'

'Then I'll tie myself to the receptionist's computer until they give us another one. Go on a hunger strike. Hire a brass band and march up and down outside until they see you.'

They'd had to wait another hour in the reception area for an appointment that lasted less than five minutes. It only took that long to confirm a pregnancy these days. Outside they'd sat on a stone step, in the sunshine, not speaking, just gripping each other's hands and smiling at each other and at everyone who walked past.

On the plane, a hitch with the seating arrangements meant she was in a different section from the rest of the tour group. She didn't mind. She took every distraction on offer. She watched five movies, one after the other. She ate everything put in front of her. She drank red wine. She left in the earphones when the movies finished, hoping they could block the thoughts.

'Shelley, at least send me emails. Let me know where you'll be.'

She could barely look at him. It hurt too much. *'Harry, there's no point. Please, can't you accept —'*

'An email. Just now and again.'

'It has to be over. We have to make a clean start. Away from each other.' How else could they recover from something like this? It wasn't a normal fight.

*

64

London was the first stop. The sky was grey, the weather cool, even though it was spring. They visited Big Ben, took a cruise down the Thames, stood outside Buckingham Palace discussing whether the Queen really was inside.

The guide called her. 'Shelley? Come on, the bus is waiting.'

'Sorry.' She'd been looking at a couple further down the footpath, peering through the gates into the palace like everyone else. The woman was her age. The man was about Harry's age. About their height too. There was a pram between them. The father's hand kept absently reaching into the pram and stroking his son or daughter's head.

Two nights in Paris. A joke party with everyone wearing berets and an impromptu quiz. The tour guide was good at impromptu activities. Name three famous French people. Shelley couldn't. She could name three French restaurants in Melbourne. She could remember three meals she'd had with Harry in those restaurants, one for their first date, the second when they got engaged. The third for no reason at all.

She could remember telling him in detail about something funny that had happened at work and him interrupting her. *'I love you very much, you know.'*

'You're dropping it into the conversation? Just like that?'

'Just like that. Sorry, go on.'

*

In Amsterdam she followed the group down the canal paths, through the red-light district, into the clog factory and the cheese shops. The guide was talking but Shelley was remembering different conversations and attempted explanations.

'I don't understand. I get home from work and you tell me it's over. You're moving out. Without even talking about it with me?'

She didn't understand herself. *'I need the space, Harry.'*

'It's not about that, is it?'

It was about the pain she felt every time she looked at him. She was trying to get as far as she could from that, not from him.

Venice. City of love. City of food. The forty members of the tour group took up three long tables in the cheery restaurant. The waiters were friendly. There was no European snobbishness. 'We're worth too much to them,' the guide had whispered to Shelley as they walked in.

'And here for poor tired Shelley who has had a long week and needs to spend the weekend with her feet up being spoiled is a glass of shockingly expensive Italian wine and the speciality of the house, crostata di pastore, *colloquially known as shepherd's pie —'*

She needed to remember the bad times, not the good times.

'*You're running away, that's what you're doing.*'

He was right. She was running away as fast as she could. But she wasn't getting anywhere. Everything that made her feel bad had come with her.

Rome. She wanted to be pinched. She stood hopefully in Piazza Navona. She watched confident, curvy Italian women walk past, watched the promenade – the *passagiata*, the guide told them. The women glanced over their shoulders, knowing they were being watched.

She remembered him walking in and finding her standing side-on in front of the full-length mirror in their bedroom. '*Is it showing yet, do you think?*'

Harry coming up behind her, with a pillow, putting it in front of her, the two of them laughing. '*Now it is.*' He grabbed another pillow. '*It might be twins.*' A third pillow. '*Triplets, even.*'

The guide organised football and basketball matches in Madrid. Shelley didn't play. She sat on a wooden bench back from the park.

*

'*You need to relax. Promise me you won't do anything while I'm away.*'

'*Sit still for three days? Harry, I'll go mad. And I want to get the room painted while I can still move.*'

'*It'll wait. I'll do it when I get back.*'

'*It'll take me less than a day.*'

'*But should you be doing all that sort of climbing around?*'

'*I'll be fine.*'

She'd been up and down the ladder, moving the chest of drawers, wriggling the cupboard side to side across the floor, wincing at the screeches it made on the floorboards, out to the car, carrying in heavy pots of paint, singing to the radio. She'd felt a twinge, so attuned to every movement in her body. Then another. Then something worse.

It was all over by the time Harry got home, even though he'd left the conference centre the second he heard her voice on the phone.

Hands held in front of a doctor the next day, but this time no smiles.

She'd asked the question. '*Doctor, did I make it happen?*'

He was an old doctor. He hadn't looked at her, making notes as he spoke, pulling open a drawer beside him, taking out a fresh prescription pad. '*I can't say. It mightn't have helped.*'

Outside, at home, the next day, the day after, the week after, they discussed it, over and over. '*He said it* mightn't *have* helped. He didn't say you killed your own child.'

'But I did. It's what you think, isn't it? You think I killed him.'

'Shell, I don't.'

'That's what you think every time you look at me.' It was what she felt every time she looked at herself in the mirror.

'Shell, I —'

She couldn't listen to the rest. She could see it in his eyes. He didn't want it to be that way, but she knew that's what he thought.

In Munich she came across a carpet shop that wouldn't have looked out of place in Morocco. The rest of the group were in a beer hall. She'd run out of things to say to them, and they had run out of things to say to her. She wanted to tell them that a year ago she would have been different, a year ago she would have loved this. Two years ago she and Harry might have been on a trip like this together. But she couldn't find the words. She hadn't been able to find the right words for anything for three months.

There was a deep-red carpet in the front window. It had a purple and green border of flowers and leaves. The longer she looked at it, the more she found hidden in the pattern. It wasn't as beautiful as their rug at home. It was the only thing she had taken with her. The carpet that had been in the hallway of their house. She'd found it in a second-hand shop a week before their wedding. It had come with a spiel from the shop owner, a second-generation Afghani. The patterns signified the future, happiness, growth. She and Harry had made love on it that night. At first on the rug itself but then it had tickled and started to burn and then she'd got the giggles. So he had put a quilt on it. She wasn't fanciful enough to think that's when their baby had been conceived. The timing was wrong. It had been a practice run.

The rug didn't look as good in her new flat. It looked out of place. It didn't quite fit. The edges pushed up against the sides of the hallway.

In Prague the bus driver tried to make a pass at her. He'd had too much wine at dinner.

'Isn't this against the company rules?' she said.

'To hell with the rules. There's something special about you.'

She'd heard him say the same thing to one of the other girls the previous night. For a moment she gave in. This was what she needed. A new experience, the feel of a different body, to cancel out and cover over memories of Harry's body. The bus driver was a good kisser. That made it easy at the start and easy for a little while. It would have been simple to sink into it, to let feeling take over from thinking even for just an hour. To cover the traces. To try and forget about everything. But when his hands strayed beneath her shirt, against her skin, it was like she was burnt. She pushed him away.

'I'm sorry, I can't. I'm married.'

'Come on. No one comes on these tours if they're married.'

'I'm separated, I mean.'

'Then you're not married, are you?'

She still felt married.

Back in London she heard music in shops, from car radios, that reminded her of him. She saw places she'd heard sung about. She imagined Harry seeing them with her. She bought a CD for him. She would send it to him. No, he had the key to her flat, he was keeping an eye on it. He'd insisted. She'd give it to him when they met after she'd got back. A thank you. A farewell present.

'Let me be sad with you. It was my baby too.'

'But you didn't hurt it like I did.'

'You didn't hurt it. It wasn't the right time for it. We'll try again.'

'We can't. We can't go backwards.'

'Then we'll go forwards. Don't give up on me.'

In Edinburgh there was a free afternoon of shopping time. On the second floor of a large shopping centre she found herself at the entrance to a Mothercare store. She had avoided any babywear shops since it happened. She would leave a shopping centre if she saw on the directory that there was one inside. This one surprised her.

In a basket in front was a collection of pale yellow, pale blue, pale pink and creamy white knitwear. Little booties. Little hats. It came up from deep inside her, the hurt and the anguish and the sorrow and the guilt. There, in a strange city, she cried for the first time. The same woman who was embarrassed if she discovered she'd walked around town with a ladder in her stocking, now standing in public, in the middle of a shopping centre, crying hard. Sobbing. The younger girl inside the store looked shocked. An older woman didn't.

'Come in here with me, pet.'

There was a small room at the back of the store. The woman didn't need to ask. She seemed to know. She handed Shelley a cup of hot tea.

'When did it happen, lovie?'

'Three months ago.'

'How old?'

'He wasn't born yet. I was five months pregnant.'

The woman nodded.

'We thought we were over the danger time. We thought we had nothing to worry about.'

'He was your first child?'

Shelley nodded.

'Is your husband all right?'

A pause. 'We separated.'

'Not for good.'

'It was my fault.'

'It wasn't your fault. It was nobody's fault, not yours, not his. Nobody's. I know.'

Shelley looked at her.

'Five times,' the woman said.

'Five miscarriages?' At the woman's nod. 'Did you ever . . .'

'One daughter, just when I'd given up hope. And she's had five children. I'm supergran. Keep talking to him, pet. Keep loving him. He needs you as much as you need him. The two of you made this baby together, so the two of you have to grieve together. Where is he?'

'At home.'

'Here in Edinburgh?'

'Australia.'

'Go home to him.'

'I'm on a tour.'

'Go home to him.'

'Promise me you'll email. I need to know you're all right. Let me collect you at least.'

She sent it from a crammed Internet café. She didn't know if he was checking his emails regularly. She wasn't due home for another five days. He'd be expecting her to go on to other parts of Scotland. He had the itinerary. He'd said he needed to have it, to know where she was. She could remember everything he had said to her and she could remember everything she had said to him.

Her plane arrived at Melbourne Airport before dawn. The queue was long through passport control, through baggage reclaim, through the double doors out into the airport. Dozens of people were waiting. There was no sign of him. He wasn't in the line of people pressed against the barrier. He wasn't there with a cardboard sign with her name written on it. He wasn't in the group of people near the door having cigarettes, or outside, double-parked in their old Holden station wagon, ready to whisk her away.

He was under the meeting-point sign. He was standing on a rug. Her rug. Their rug.

She was crying as she moved towards him. His arms were open. She moved into them and pressed her face against his chest.

'I'm so sorry, Harry.'

'Welcome home, Shelley.' He didn't say anything else. Not yet. He just held her tighter.

The Role Model

When I look back at those strange, sad months of last year, it's as if we had joined a cult. Four sensible women in our late thirties, friends since school, but somehow, without noticing, we lost our reason and perspective, and so much else as well.

It began with the arrival in our town of the new doctor and his wife. He was comfortingly like the old doctor: in his early fifties, short dark hair, kind face. The sort of man you wouldn't look twice at in the street, which was a relief when you had to undress in front of him in the surgery. His wife, however, was something else. Tall, fine-featured, slender as a model, beautifully groomed, and at least twenty years younger than him, which made her just a few years younger than the four of us.

Our town was a small one, with the usual amenities: one main street of shops, two pubs, three schools, a small hospital and a good medical centre that served the communities for one hundred kilometres around. There was little to distinguish it from dozens of other Australian country towns apart from its proximity to a large lake, which meant for several months of the year it became a holiday haven. We were used to our country lives being invaded by the city-ites, as we called them, but they never raised any envy among us. It was like watching migratory birds fly in, make a lot of noise and leave. When my three friends and I met for our usual Saturday-morning coffee at one of the lakeside cafés, we liked to guess at the amount of money these holidaying women had spent on their clothes or shoes or swimsuits, but they didn't bother us. We knew they'd be gone soon and we could go back to our own lives.

Caitlyn, the doctor's wife, was different. She was here to stay. Caitlyn, with her designer wardrobe, sleek hair, close-fitting clothes and the something else that we couldn't quite put our fingers on. Aloofness, my friend Jenny called it. Stuck-up-ness, Susan called it. Snobbery, Alice said. I was undecided at first. Maybe she was just shy, I suggested.

'Shy? She's got more confidence in her little finger than I have in my whole body. And as you can all see, I have a lot of body.' Susan was an ample size 18, curvaceous and brown-skinned. 'I've asked her over for coffee three times, and she's cancelled each time, said she wasn't feeling well. The last time she cancelled I saw her an hour later, picking up her husband in their car – a new model Mercedes, of course – and she looked fine. She saw me, I know she did, and she looked away. Guilt written all over her face.'

'You're just jealous of her.' We'd been friends long enough to speak the truth like that. But Susan still took offence.

'Jealous of what?'

'Her figure. Her looks. Her relationship with her husband.'

Susan poked out her tongue. She used to do that to me at school too. It meant my words had hit home, even if she wouldn't admit it.

The truth was we were all a bit jealous of Caitlyn's relationship with her husband. We'd all seen them talking over dinner in the town's one high-class restaurant, her leaning her head on his shoulder, him stroking the hair from her face, holding her hand, as though she was some precious object. When we went out with our husbands, we went as a group. They talked to each other about sport and business while the four of us talked about every other single thing. As for public displays of affection, forget it. The idea of going out with our husbands, in pairs, was out of the question too. People in the town would think the 'Gang of Four', as we were known, had had a falling-out.

'They must be newlyweds,' Jenny suggested.

'They're not,' Susan said. 'They've been married for ten years. Her husband told the receptionist at the medical centre who told her sister who told me. They had their anniversary just last week.'

'Where did he find her? The local primary school?'

'She's older than she looks. Thirty-four, I was told.' Susan was very good at finding out people's personal details. She worked part-time in the council office and had access to a large database. She swore she never looked up information on any of us, but I wondered sometimes.

Alice sniffed. 'She'd better get a move on with the kids, then.'

The fact Caitlyn didn't have children created another barrier, in a way. The four of us had seven kids between us, ranging in age from ten to fifteen. We'd had to put a ban on talking about them at our coffee mornings, otherwise the time would have gone before we'd even started on our husbands.

By unspoken agreement, we switched the subject from Caitlyn to a different, favourite subject.

'I've been thinking about dieting again,' Alice said.

Jenny put down the last few centimetres of her croissant. 'Me too.'

'Me too.' I didn't have any of my croissant left to put down.

Susan pulled a face. 'That's all I think about. Diets and food. Food and diets. Food always wins.'

'It's the thought that counts,' I said. 'Anyway, you're beautiful just the way you are.'

I know a lot of women say that to their friends and mean it, but in our case, it was a lie. The truth was that each of us was overweight, by at least ten kilos. We had been for years, since we started having children, not finding time to exercise, excusing ourselves our morning biscuits and afternoon snacks, eating the kids' leftovers . . . The weight had just crept on, but because it had happened to all four of us, it kept us on an even keel, so to speak. Several years earlier, Jenny had got a bad stomach bug and lost nearly five kilos in two weeks. It upset the equilibrium. She'd been as anxious to put the weight back on as we were anxious for her to do it.

'I got this flyer in the post last week.' Alice held up a piece of yellow paper. She worked in the pharmacy and was a fount of knowledge on all matters medical and cultural. The pharmacy window was the display area of choice in our town, for everything from lost-dog notices to Cars 4 Sale to advertisements like this one.

The writing was black and bold:

Overweight? Over it?
CHANGE IT.

The flyer went on to explain this wasn't the usual calorie-counting deprivation regime. The instructor would go to the core of her clients' weight problems, using a new approach. Our town had been chosen for a pilot program. If anyone signed up for ten weeks, they'd get the last two weeks for free. That appealed to all of us. We'd been to enough weight-loss sessions over the years as it was, eventually tiring of handing over the price of a nice lunch to be told how much we weighed. We could do that at home for free.

We were all on time the next week for the first meeting. It

took place in the small room at the back of the medical centre. To our relief, there was only the four of us. Possibly because Alice hadn't put the flyer back up in the pharmacy window.

The instructor came in a few minutes after us. She was a petite, sharp-eyed, well-groomed woman in her sixties. She nodded a welcome.

We settled into our chairs, waiting for the pep talk, the jokes, the charts, the discussion about portion size, the shock news that there were as many calories in one glass of wine as there were in fifteen cream buns.

But there was no welcoming smile. No motivational 'I used to be overweight and now I am thin' photos. Instead, the woman briskly introduced herself as Margot – she didn't give a surname – and then left the room, returning wheeling a full-length mirror. Still unsmiling, she asked each of us to go and look at ourselves for a minute, in turn, and then sit down again.

We did, fighting back nervous giggles, not daring to look at each other, unsettled by the silence in the room.

'Have you all had a good look at yourselves?' she said after we'd sat down again. She still wasn't smiling.

We nodded.

She was silent for a few minutes, staring at each of us in turn. All our smiles had gone by now too.

When she spoke again, her voice was low, firm and cold. 'Aren't you ashamed? Embarrassed? Disgusted?'

Susan gasped.

Margot continued. 'You should be. How could you have let

yourselves go so badly?' She looked directly at me. 'Have you seen your back view? You're twice the size you should be. As for you —' she looked at Jenny, 'where is your self-respect, coming out in public wearing clothes as baggy and shapeless as that?' Another laser glare, this time at Susan. 'You must have been pretty once – what happened?' Alice wasn't excluded from the insults either. 'You're not pregnant, are you?' Alice shook her head. Another long pause. 'Well, you look it.'

This time there were four gasps, one from each of us. Susan rallied first. 'How dare you? We've come here to lose weight, not be insulted.'

'You deserve to be insulted,' Margot said in that same steely tone. 'And I'll tell you something else. You *will* lose weight with me. Because I'll say it like it is, every week, until you've lost all this lard and turned back into attractive women. Because you're not attractive at the moment, are you? You don't look it and you don't feel it, no matter how much you might pretend otherwise.'

More gasps, but somehow, just then, there was a subtle change of mood in the room. She was right.

On and on she went, in the same cold voice. She wouldn't be soft-soaping us, excusing us, making allowances. It was obviously we'd been doing that to ourselves for too long already. The same words kept coming up in her speech – weren't we ashamed, disgusted, appalled? Didn't we hate our ugly bodies, wobbly thighs, bulging stomachs? A childhood saying came back to me: *Sticks and stones may break my bones but words can never hurt me.* The saying was wrong. Words could hurt and Margot was choosing the most hurtful of them with perfect aim and precision.

She asked questions but didn't wait for our answers. She talked about our poor husbands, having to get in bed with these revolting bodies. Had we all been thin on our wedding days? Yes, we had, but she didn't wait for that answer either. On she went about our husbands, how they had every right to leave us; we weren't the women they'd married; we'd become lazy and uncaring; showing them as much disrespect as we showed our own bodies.

Mid-diatribe, something outside the window caught her attention. Not something but someone, in the car park of the medical centre. It was Caitlyn, getting into her husband's Mercedes.

'Look at her,' Margot said.

We looked.

'What has she got that you four haven't? I'll tell you. Self-respect. Self-love. That's a woman who takes care of herself, who respects herself. You can see it in her figure, in her clothes, in her make-up. But you four?'

Jenny started to cry. I was too shocked. I wanted to leave; I wanted to throw insults back at Margot, but there was something frightening and compelling about her approach.

She was telling the truth.

She glanced at Jenny, then calmly reached for her bag. 'That's all for today.'

Our shock must have shown. Susan, always the bravest, spoke up. 'How can that be all? We should sue you for false advertising. Where are the tips and the diet sheets?'

Margot fixed her with a stare. I was uncomfortably reminded of a snake staring down its prey. 'You don't need diet sheets. You're grown women. You already know why you're fat.'

That word. Fat. Not overweight, not curvy.

'You eat too much. You don't exercise. So change it. I'll see you next week.'

The door closed behind her, not with a bang or a slam, but with a firm sharp click. We were silent for a moment and then the room exploded into noise. Anger, astonishment, and even – eventually – some laughter.

'She's a witch,' Jenny said, shuddering. 'She's flown up from the underworld.'

'More of a bitch than a witch,' Susan said. 'I've never heard anything like it in my life. She can't get away with that, can she?'

'We're the ones who paid to meet her,' I said. 'She didn't force us.'

'Well, she'll be talking to an empty room next week, I'll tell you that.' Susan's expression changed as she looked at the rest of us, from outrage to surprise. 'You're not going to come back, are you?'

Another brief silence.

'It's a different approach,' I said. 'Maybe there's something in it.'

'A different approach? Insulting and offensive and belittling . . .'

'I wish she could belittle me,' Jenny said gloomily, rubbing her belly.

We laughed and a little more tension lifted. A knock at the door got us moving. Someone else needed the room. We all had to go and do shopping, pick up the kids, go back to work.

'Let's keep all of this to ourselves,' Alice said in an oddly urgent voice as we walked out together. 'We'll give her a second chance, but no one needs to know how awful she is, do they?'

That was the first mistake we made. We agreed to keep quiet.

The second week was worse, if possible. More insults. No weighing – 'You've all got scales at home, haven't you? Use them. You don't need me to tell you you're carrying too much fat.' For an hour she hit us with a barrage of insults and each one of them stayed with us.

It wasn't Caityln's fault that she happened to be walking down the main street as the four of us came out of the second meeting. Or her fault that, yet again, she was beautifully dressed, her clothes skimming her model figure, her posture perfect, her whole image so feminine and graceful. We felt like four elephants coming across a deer in a forest clearing. But – and I know I wasn't the only one to think it – seeing her again was like a sign. She was the finished product. We were the raw, unshapely materials. Margot was right. We *were* disgusting. We *were* fat. We felt like our bodies *were* revolting. But we didn't have to be like that. We could change.

Looking back, our obsession started that day. We didn't go so far as taking clandestine photos of Caitlyn and sticking them on our fridges, but we came close. If we felt ourselves slipping, reaching for the chocolate or the biscuits, we'd ring each other and talk about Caitlyn. We even developed our own dieting catchphrase around her. I was the one who coined it. At a party once, I'd met a woman wearing a necklace with the letters WWJD. I asked her what the letters stood for.

She smiled, put her hand on mine and said, 'I'm so glad you asked. It stands for What Would Jesus Do? It's how I live my life, every day, from moment to moment.'

Alice, Susan and Jenny had laughed about it when I told them afterwards. I remembered the phrase that day as we spoke enviously about Caitlyn.

'I need to spy on her,' I said. 'Live my life the Caitlyn way. Ask myself every day, moment by moment, WWCD? What Would Caitlyn Do?'

It was a joke that quickly became serious. We started living our lives by what we termed the Caitlyn creed. Would Caitlyn eat that biscuit? Of course she wouldn't. Would Caitlyn put butter on her toast? No, she would not. Would Caitlyn serve chips instead of salad? Would Caitlyn decide she was too tired to exercise? Would Caitlyn sleep in or go for an hour's walk every morning? We knew the answers. And if we kept doing what Caitlyn would do, then we would soon be as thin as her, wouldn't we?

We didn't tell Margot about Caitlyn. There was never much conversation with Margot anyway, and we certainly didn't want to draw any more attention to the perfect Caitlyn, in case Margot got it into her head to invite her to one of the meetings and parade her naked in front of us. Margot was busy enough with our four bodies. Week after week, she would pick on a particular area, force us to stand in front of the mirror and look at it, insult us, harangue us. Hips one meeting. Waists the next. Breasts after that.

We'd undressed in front of each other since we were at school together, but even so, it was slightly embarrassing to do it. The light wasn't flattering in that meeting room, even after Margot had, thankfully, drawn the curtains.

Silent and stony-faced as always, Margot would inspect each of us in turn like an army major on parade duty. We could feel her glances at our tired old bras, our stretchmarks, our bulges.

'Didn't you ever *look* at yourselves before? Realise how ugly your bodies are?'

She never encouraged us, never praised us. And yet we kept going back to her. We even upped the meetings to twice a week. Our suggestion, not hers. Why?

Because it was working.

Because all four of us were losing weight. And not just a little bit. A lot of weight. It was like some kind of miracle.

Whenever any of us reached for something sweet or fatty, or for a second helping, or for something fried, we'd hear Margot's haranguing voice, heaping scorn on our bodies, insulting us. That voice, combined with a mental picture of who we wanted to be – Caitlyn – was more powerful to us than diet pills, gym memberships and weekly weigh-ins put together.

Our husbands started to notice a change. Our kids noticed, first that the cakes, biscuits and chips had disappeared from our houses, second that we had stopped driving them everywhere and were making them walk instead. Shop assistants, other friends and our relatives noticed. The more comments we got, the more driven we became, the more obsessed we grew – with our bodies and, increasingly, with Caitlyn.

We'd call each other if there was a Caitlyn sighting, discussing in forensic detail her figure, her hair, her shoes, her accessories. We'd also ring if we'd managed to dress in a pair of jeans or a skirt long-consigned to the back of the wardrobe. We still met every Saturday morning, but only for a quick black coffee before we did an hour's walk together around the lake. We did that walk every day, sometimes even twice a day.

As the weight kept disappearing, some of the compliments from our families and friends turned to concern. Questions were asked. Were we on diet pills? Had we had liposuction? What was going on? Was it healthy to lose so much, so quickly? We became very skilled at deflecting their questions. We kept quiet about Margot's methods, just murmured about feeling extra-motivated with summer coming, tired of having trouble finding clothes to wear, the usual reasons. We didn't want anyone else coming to Margot's meetings.

I often wonder if Caitlyn had any idea how obsessed we all were with her. I'd see her in the supermarket, or walking down the main street, or out with her husband. She smiled at me once or twice, a nice, shy, inviting smile. I could have started a conversation with her. Invited her and her husband out for a drink. But I didn't. How could I talk to her about ordinary things like the weather, or something in the news? She wasn't an ordinary woman any more. To Alice, Susan, Jenny and I, she'd become the equivalent of Cindy Crawford or Elle Macpherson living in our town. We could look at her, yes, but talk to her? No way. What could we possibly say? Why would she be interested in us? She was the perfect one; we were the imperfect ones. But we were working hard to close the gap.

The weeks went by. Two months after that first meeting with Margot, we had each dropped nearly three dress sizes.

We were seriously the talk of the town. 'What's your secret?' 'You all look so great.' People who had never dared suggest we had weight to lose were boldly telling us how much better we looked now we were thinner. Each word of praise was more motivation.

Then Caitlyn went away. It took us four days to notice and another day to find out for sure. Yes, she and the doctor had gone on holiday. Margot's meetings went on, the insults as bad, the competition between us as fierce, the weight loss as sought after, but something was missing. Someone. Our motivation. Her.

To our amazement, Margot noticed we were distracted. 'What's wrong with you four?'

Out it poured. We told her all about Caitlyn being our talisman – or taliswoman. Our idol. We were sheepish about it, expecting to be admonished. We were admonished about everything else, after all. But Margot approved. She asked us to describe her, and nodded thoughtfully, saying she recalled seeing her that day in the car park.

'You've made a good choice. I remember her. Elegant, thin, well groomed. And so can all of you be. If you keep that greed of yours at bay and keep taking good hard looks at yourselves, that is. You're only halfway there, you know. You think you're thinner, but each of you still has a serious weight problem. When will this Caitlyn be back?'

We didn't know but we wanted – needed – to find out. Jenny made an appointment with one of the other doctors on false pretences, finishing the consultation with an apparently cheery, innocent enquiry about the new doctor and his wife and when they might be due back from holiday.

'We're not sure,' he said.

We were outraged. How could they not be sure? Typical doctors, taking holidays when it suited them. Didn't they realise we *needed* Caitlyn?

Nearly two weeks later, we saw her again. At least I saw

her, and rang the others. We all made excuses to get down to the main street as soon as we could, before she finished her shopping.

The first thing we noticed was that she looked different. She had a new, shorter hairstyle for starters. But even the shape of her face had changed. Her cheekbones were more pronounced, her skin even paler, her lipstick a bold red. She looked like Audrey Hepburn or a Parisian model. And not only that. We didn't know how she had managed it, but there was no escaping it. She was even thinner than before.

Susan asked around and got all the answers. Caitlyn and her husband had been to a spa in Indonesia, she reported back to us. One of those five-star luxury places. She'd obviously had the works. Colonic irrigation. Botox. Fasting. Mudwraps and facepacks and seaweed baths. Some sort of collagen implants too, judging by those new cheekbones.

We weren't just envious now, we were angry. That was unfair. That was shifting the goalposts. We could afford to eat less and do more exercise – doing that saved us money, in fact – but we couldn't head away to some glamorous resort to be pampered and fussed over and operated on.

Something changed in all of us then. We turned on Caitlyn. All four of us. Alice had always liked to gossip, but she wasn't usually vicious about it. Yet she started being spiteful about Caitlyn, suggesting she was a gold-digger, had a father-figure complex, that there was something, well, a little bit *creepy*, didn't we think, about her husband being so much older than her? Once it was said, it changed the way we viewed her and the doctor when we saw them out together. What had been a source of envy to us – their whispered conversations, his attentiveness, the public displays of affection – now looked sordid.

Word went around, fuelled by gossip – from us – that Caitlyn was even younger than we thought. A rumour started that she had actually once been engaged to the doctor's son, and had then set her sights on the doctor himself. It wasn't true, of course. I don't even know where that story came from. Not from us, I know that. But once it aired, it was out there and there was no way of getting it back. It grew into other stories, travelling around the town, increasing in size and detail each time we heard it. She'd actually gone away to Sydney, not Bali, and not on holiday but to have an abortion. She'd told her husband she never wanted to have kids and she meant it. No, another rumour announced, it *was* a holiday, but it was because their marriage was in trouble and it was a last effort to stay together. Then someone else said they'd seen the doctor's son in town, all three of them out dining together. Was it a *ménage à trois*?

As the gossip swirled around the town, we saw Caitlyn less and less. I spotted her in the main street one afternoon and actually crossed the road to avoid passing her. I told myself that I needed to keep a distance, to keep her on that pedestal, to keep my goals intact.

A month later the doctor and Caitlyn went away again.

Another holiday, Alice heard. Well, so what? we told ourselves. We didn't need her any more. We kept paying Margot
to insult us twice a week. She had put up her prices but we'd
have paid whatever she wanted by this stage. I was now a
size 12 for the first time in my life. Jenny and Susan had lost
fifteen kilos each. Alice was winning, down sixteen kilos, but
then she had had the most to lose. We bought new clothes. We
flaunted our new bodies. We barely ate anything any more.
We were too busy exercising. We told each other we had never
been so happy.

I was at home when I heard the news. Jenny rang me. I had
to ask her to tell me three times before I believed it.

'Dead? Caitlyn's *dead*?'

I asked Jenny all the questions she had been asking people
too. How? An accident? When? Where? There's no mistake?
Caitlyn's *dead*?

Jenny didn't know any more details. She'd heard it from her
cousin who had heard it from the medical centre receptionist
who'd taken the call from the doctor's son. No details, just
the basic facts.

If there had been a swirl of gossip about Caitlyn before this,
there was now a hurricane. It was a car accident; the doctor
had been drink-driving. No, she was a drug addict and she'd
overdosed. No, it was suicide. No, the doctor had killed her
and was now covering it up.

I didn't go to Margot's meeting the morning after I heard
the news. The others did. They were as shocked by the news

about Caitlyn as I was, but they still went. Jenny rang me straight afterwards. I listened, but only barely. They'd told Margot about Caitlyn. That the perfect specimen, the role model she'd held up to us, was dead.

'Do you know what she said then?' Jenny was crying.

I didn't answer. I didn't want to hear what Margot might have said.

'She said, "Sad, yes, but it doesn't change the way she looked when she was alive. Keep that image in your minds. That's your goal."'

None of us went to the funeral. It was held in a town a hundred kilometres away, where Caitlyn had grown up and where she would be buried. I didn't hear any details about it until the following week.

I had decided to go back to Margot's meetings. I thought it would focus me again. I was finding it hard to care about dieting and exercise any more. I needed that hectoring voice in my ear: 'Hate the body you're in. Love the body you'll get.'

I was early, for once. The others weren't there yet. As I waited, the receptionist came into the room with some files. We got talking. About Caitlyn, unsurprisingly. The receptionist had been to the funeral, she told me. It was beautiful. A celebration of her life, the way a good funeral should be. Her husband had given the eulogy.

'Everyone was crying by the end. He loved her so much.'

'How did it happen?' I asked, choosing my words carefully in case it had been an overdose, or suicide. I had to know. The rumours were still flying and the truth hadn't reached our ears yet.

She looked at me as if I was a bit stupid. 'Her cancer came back.'

'Caitlyn had cancer?'

'That's how they met. He was doing a research paper about her. That's why they moved here.'

I don't remember the questions I must have asked, but I soon knew the story of Caitlyn's life. She was diagnosed with breast cancer in her early twenties. She had fought it with chemotherapy, lifestyle changes, determination and won. It was how she and her husband had met, the year she turned twenty-three. Already divorced from his first wife, single and a workaholic, he'd been undertaking research into alternative cancer treatments. They had fallen in love. Yes, they had both always known there was the possibility the disease could return, but they lived life well and joyously. Eighteen months previously, there was a bad test result. They decided to change their lives. They moved to a country town. Our town. Hoping the slower pace of life, the fresh air, living in a close-knit, friendly community could help Caitlyn. Close-knit community? We had barely spoken to Caitlyn. As for help her . . .

The receptionist told me there were attempts to fight the cancer with trials of new drugs. Visits to alternative-therapy centres in Bali. Attempts to live a normal life. That's why people hadn't been told. Caitlyn had wanted friendship, not sympathy.

The doctor's eulogy had been so honest and so sad, the

woman said. He'd spoken of the two of them realising that this time her body wasn't strong enough to fight it again. He talked about his love for her spirit, her humour, her zest for living, her kindness, her gentleness. Of how much he would miss her. Of how much she had meant to him. Of the plans they had made together, the children they had longed to have together, the memories they had still managed to make.

Even as I listened, my own thoughts were crashing into my head, the pieces falling into place, the real story of Caitlyn pushing out the fantasy we had created around her.

Caitlyn wasn't thin because she dieted. She was thin because she was so ill. She hadn't changed her hair for fashion reasons. She'd bought a wig to cover her baldness, a side effect of her treatment. Her husband hadn't cared for her so tenderly because it was a winter–spring romance. It was because he knew better than anyone that she was not going to be with him for very long. Each of those loving glances, those romantic dinners, had been precious moments in a long, sad, drawn-out farewell to the woman he loved. Those shy, inviting smiles she had given me had indeed been that – invitations to be her friend. And I had ignored them.

I left the medical centre then, before the others arrived.

I never went back to Margot's meetings again. Jenny went for one more week, before leaving midway through, calling me, barely able to speak for her tears. She came to my house to talk, rather than to the café. We didn't want any comments about our weight, our new bodies, our new looks.

She said that afternoon all that I had already decided. That it felt wrong to sit in a room, to be healthy and alive and yet be told to hate our bodies, our strong, healthy bodies. To hate our legs that had carried us throughout our lives, to hate our bellies and our breasts that had grown and nurtured our children. To think of food as the enemy and our bodies as battlegrounds when we should be celebrating our bodies and our lives every day.

Jenny and I decided I'd be the one to tell Alice, Susan and Margot that we didn't want to go to the meetings any more. Three times I tried to call them. Each time I put down the phone. In the end I wrote notes. Cowardly to the last, I didn't tell the truth. I said Jenny and I were too busy. Perhaps that wasn't a lie. We had decided to get busy. Busy being glad we were alive and enjoying all the good things that we could, while we could.

That was six months ago. Alice and Susan still go to Margot's meetings. Jenny and I heard that we'd been replaced by two other women within a week. Word spread. There are now twenty women attending the two meetings each week. I heard that Alice is planning on setting up her own group. I don't know for sure. Alice and Susan don't really talk to Jenny and me any more.

We see them quite often, though. It's a small town; it's hard to avoid each other. The most recent encounter was yesterday. Jenny and I had organised a picnic beside the lake, with our husbands, our kids and several other friends, including a new couple who recently moved to town. I met the woman in a queue at the post office. Where once I would have left it at that – a conversation about the weather – that day I took the extra step of inviting her for a coffee. She'd accepted even before I'd finished delivering the invitation. Since then we've socialised together at least once or twice a week.

I'd done the baking for the picnic – oatmeal biscuits and the sultana cupcakes my kids love. I used less butter than I might have in the old days, but they still tasted delicious.

We'd just set out all the food and drink on the picnic rugs by the lake when Alice, Susan and five other women went jogging past. They looked great. Thinner than slim, tanned and toned muscles, fashionably dressed in designer exercise wear. They waved at us and Jenny and I waved back, sitting there surrounded by food. I knew what they were thinking and they knew what we were thinking. Jenny and I didn't need to say anything about them after they'd gone, though. We'd done that enough, for hours, talking about how guilty we felt, and how we hoped we would never let something like that take us over again.

I reached into the picnic basket behind me, took out the thermoses for the adults and the bottles of juice for the kids and passed around the sandwiches, cakes and biscuits. After lunch, we got up and played a game of cricket together, enjoying a beautiful day with family and friends.

I hope that's what Caitlyn would have done.

Wedding Fever

Since Jeannie had started cleaning houses to help pay her way through university, she'd stopped watching television soaps. There'd been so much drama in her real life she didn't need fictional versions any more.

She'd posted advertisements in bookshop windows in Richmond, Carlton and Hawthorn promising reliable, meticulous cleaning using only natural, chemical-free products. It was a great lure, she discovered – people who felt guilty about hiring a cleaner didn't have to feel guilty for destroying the planet too. Her clients so far had included a professional couple who communicated only via a series of bad-tempered notes, a family of five who appeared to throw their food at the wall rather than eat it, three untidy lawyers with immaculate wardrobes and possible drug habits and an old man with a big libido who'd chased her around the living room until she'd hit him with her mop.

She had good references from her pre-university jobs (teacher's aide, library assistant and swimming-pool attendant), but no one ever asked to see them, or indeed asked her anything about herself. That surprised her. If she'd been in a position to have someone come into her house and clean, she'd have liked to know a little more about them.

'That's because you're the most curious woman on the planet,' her ex-boyfriend Richard had said. 'It's mad, Jeannie. You've got brains to burn, and you're cleaning other people's bathrooms. Why don't you temp, at least? Get an office job somewhere?'

She liked cleaning. It kept her fit, especially as she rode her bike from job to job as well. And it was a means to an end. Once she got teaching qualifications, her options would be much wider. But Richard wouldn't see it from her point of view. That had been one of his biggest faults, she'd sadly discovered. Three months ago, after a particularly big disagreement, she'd called it off between them.

It had been a very lonely time. She'd distracted herself by studying harder and taking on as many cleaning jobs as possible. The previous night she'd had a phone call from another prospective client, a woman in Carlton.

'Would you be interested in a regular position? In two regular positions, in fact? Could you drop around and talk to me about them?'

Jeannie easily found the address the following day. It was a small cottage in need of a coat of paint, but still charming.

A smiling woman in her mid-twenties answered the door and introduced herself as Kate. Following her down the polished timber-floor hallway, Jeannie noticed coffee and biscuits on the kitchen table. She also picked up a strong smell of furniture polish. Like many of Jeannie's first-time clients, Kate had obviously cleaned the house before her arrival.

After agreeing on payment rates and cleaning times, Jeannie gently told Kate she didn't need to clean beforehand next time. 'I'm happy for you to leave it to me, really.' She smiled. 'Have bicarb, will clean.'

Kate looked quite relieved. 'Isn't it harder for you, though, all that extra scrubbing?'

She was the first person to ask Jeannie that question. Jeannie's other clients had been more concerned that soda and vinegar actually did the job. 'A bit, but I've got the best biceps in Melbourne now.' She flexed a brown arm.

'And you're studying at the uni, you said? Are you from here originally?'

The mobile phone on the table rang before Jeannie could answer. Kate apologised before taking what was obviously a work call. She'd already explained to Jeannie that she worked from home as a fundraiser for local charities. When she hung up, she'd forgotten they'd been in mid-conversation. Jeannie didn't mind. She preferred to work, not talk about herself. She pulled on her gloves, took out her cleaning cloths and got cracking.

An hour later she'd just finished when she heard Kate on

the phone again. 'She's brilliant, Sam, thanks so much again.'
She hung up and joined Jeannie, still smiling. 'That was my
fiancé. He's the reason you're here, actually. It's turned out to
be a really busy time at work and Sam was worried I was getting a bit stressed, trying to do too much. You're his wedding
present to me.'

'Not the only one, I hope?'

Kate grinned. 'Well, he did say something about a wedding
ring too, but we'll see.'

'Congratulations – when's the big day?'

She named a date two months away, then hesitated. 'Big is
the right word, as it happens. My sister's getting married on
the same day.'

'A double wedding? How lovely.'

Kate nodded. 'Yes. Yes, it's great.'

Jeannie noticed straightaway that it wasn't great. Kate's
voice was too bright, her smile not reaching her eyes.

She barely needed to ask another question. Kate seemed
eager, anxious even, to tell her the whole story. She'd known
Sam for eight years, been engaged for three, she told Jeannie.
They'd taken it slowly, saving for their own house, the wedding, a long honeymoon.

'My parents got divorced when Amanda and I were teenagers, so I didn't take getting married lightly. I needed to be
sure. And I wanted our wedding to be exactly what we both
wanted. Relaxed and fun.'

'And then your sister just happened to pick the same day?'

Kate shifted position, crossing her arms in front of her. Jeannie wondered what a body language expert would make of that. 'It was a whirlwind romance. He's a stockbroker, she's an executive secretary, they met at a charity function. He proposed on the third date. And Amanda, well, when she gets an idea in her head . . . She called us all together, even Dad, and announced she didn't want a long engagement like me. That she wanted to get married as soon as possible. Before me, if necessary.' Kate bit her lip, looking very young for a moment. Jeannie could only guess at the family drama that would have sparked. 'My father came up with the solution in the end. Have it on the same day.'

'And you didn't mind?'

'Oh no.' Again, the voice too bright. 'It makes sense, doesn't it? We both want to be married. No point going to all that fuss twice in just a few weeks, as my mother said.'

All that fuss? Jeannie's heart went out to Kate. No one wanted their wedding to be described as 'all that fuss'.

'It's actually my sister who wants to employ you as well. The second job I mentioned. Her regular cleaner left her in the lurch, she said, and when I told her about your ad, she asked me to check you out and if —' she stopped, embarrassed.

'If I was any good to send me to her as well?'

Kate nodded, still looking uncomfortable. 'She's quite pernickety.'

'Pernickety?' Jeannie laughed. It sounded like a word out of a fairytale.

'Very pernickety,' Kate said gloomily.

Meeting Amanda the following day at her large apartment in a tree-lined South Yarra street, Jeannie thought of fairytales again. The sisters were like Snow White and Rose Red: Amanda's hair as dark, straight and shiny as Kate's was soft, wavy and blonde. Five minutes into the interview, Jeannie decided pernickety wasn't the word for Amanda. Bossy, perhaps. Imperious. Most definitely self-absorbed. Amanda told Jeannie which day suited her (Monday), what hours she wanted Jeannie to work ('You should be able to manage it in two hours. My old cleaner could and she didn't look half as fit as you do') and the order she wanted the rooms cleaned ('Start from the front door and work your way in, would you? I hate the smell of cleaning products when I come home.')

As she stood up, she nodded disparagingly towards Jeannie's bag of natural cleaning products. 'Do they actually work?'

'With a bit of elbow grease, yes, they're great.'

'Grease? On these white carpets?'

Jeannie decided to change the subject. 'Kate tells me you're getting married soon too. Congratulations.'

Amanda's expression changed, from frown to radiant smile. 'It's so wonderful. I've always dreamed of it. My own special day.'

'But isn't it a double wedding? You and Kate?'

Amanda's chin went up. 'I know she was engaged first, but I couldn't wait. And we still get to have what each of us wants.'

Jeannie had been wondering about that. 'If you don't

mind me asking, how does it work? Do you decorate half the church each, choose half the reception menu, decide on half the flowers?'

Amanda looked appalled. 'Good God, no. We'll do it all my way, of course.' She gave a quick, sharp laugh. 'I'm joking. We'll compromise. It'll be a great day for us both.' She picked up her large handbag. 'I'll leave you to it.'

Over the next few weeks, as Jeannie moved back and forth between the two sisters' houses, she began to feel more like a counsellor than a cleaner. Under normal circumstances, as she knew herself, it was difficult to be within ten feet of a bride and not get swept up in their wedding plans. This, however, wasn't a normal wedding, even by double wedding standards. It was a battle.

She heard everything from Kate. Her updates over their now-regular coffee together were like tuning into a weekly TV soap opera. If a disagreement on any aspect of the wedding was possible, it seemed Amanda, Kate and their mother were managing it. Both sisters had declared they would pay for their own weddings, refusing to accept anything from their parents. The difficulty was Amanda – or more accurately, Amanda's fiancé – had much more money than Kate and her fiancé. Not only were their budgets different, but so were the sisters' tastes. Amanda wanted a fairytale dress, six bridesmaids, imported white roses, floral arches, French champagne and a full choir. Kate wanted a simple white shift dress, no bridesmaids, jonquils, sparkling wine and a violinist. Their mother wanted perfect symmetry: four bridesmaids each, matching lilac flowers and dresses, elaborate food and expensive wine.

It was no surprise to come into Kate's cottage one morning to find her crying. She leapt up from the sofa as Jeannie came in, wiping away her tears, embarrassed. 'Oh Jeannie, I'm sorry. I know it shouldn't matter so much, but I can't help it. Would you take a look? It is awful, isn't it? It's not just me being difficult?'

Jeannie looked. It was a computer mock-up of a church altar and a reception room. It looked like Las Vegas mated with Disneyland: huge floral arches, fake doves suspended in mid-air, gold and silver balloons in the shape of cherubs . . .

Jeannie did her best to hide her feelings. 'This is what Amanda wants?'

'No, this is her *compromise*. It's taken us three weeks to get to this.' Kate looked like she didn't know whether she wanted to laugh or cry. The tears won. 'I've never understood her. It's always been like this, all our lives. If I got a toy for my birthday, she'd want a bigger one for hers. If I got good marks at school, she had to get better ones. I saved and saved to buy this cottage, she had to buy a bigger apartment. And now even my wedding day. It's as if she deliberately went out and found a rich fiancé so she could try and beat me at this too. Not that I care that he's richer than Sam. Richer than Sam and I put together. Money's not important to me, it never was. Or to Sam. We just knew what we wanted on our wedding day, and now between her and my mother, it's all, oh, I don't know . . .'

Jeannie found herself saying words she'd only recently heard herself. 'Getting taken away from you? Turning into someone else's day, not yours?'

'That's it. That's it exactly.' Kate stood up then, roughly wiping away the tears, picking up the print-out. 'Sam will go crazy when he sees this. He thought it was funny at the start. But he keeps saying he never wants to hear about a pew decoration or table setting again. That this isn't about our wedding any more, it's about showing off.'

Jeannie had that feeling of *déjà vu* again. It was an uncomfortable feeling. 'He'll come round, though, won't he?'

'Will he?' Kate gave an unhappy sigh. 'I just don't know, Jeannie. I really don't.'

The following week, Jeannie let herself into Amanda's flat and found her in the middle of the living room, weeping noisily. A round-faced balding man several inches shorter than her was holding her tight, trying to soothe her. When Jeannie had imagined Amanda's fiancé Ivan, he hadn't looked like this.

With brimming eyes and tear-streaked cheeks, Amanda introduced him. She looked so unhappy Jeannie almost felt sorry for her. 'Would you both rather I came back later?'

'No, stay. The house is a mess.' Amanda took a shuddering

breath. 'Have you seen Kate lately? Has she told you why she's doing this? It's to get back at me, isn't it?'

Jeannie just blinked.

'She's doing it deliberately, isn't she? She's always been jealous of me and now she's ruining my wedding, refusing to accept any of my designs, not even one. After I'd compromised and *everything*.'

'Shh, shh.' Ivan rubbed Amanda's back again.

Amanda started to cry again. 'It's not fair, Ivan. I knew exactly what I wanted and now I can't have it. Because of her. She's so selfish.' A torrent of complaints poured out. Everything was ruined. All she wanted was her dream day, the day she and Ivan wanted, it was their special day —

Before she quite knew where the words had come from, Jeannie interrupted. 'Why don't you elope?'

'— just because she got engaged first, she —' Amanda stared. 'What did you just say?'

Jeannie was having trouble believing she'd said it too. 'I just wondered, have you thought about eloping?'

Amanda's eyes narrowed. 'Has Kate told you to say this?'

'No, she hasn't. It's completely my own idea.' That wasn't exactly true, but this wasn't the time to go into it.

'But everyone would be so disappointed. All my friends. They've been dying to see my dress and my tiara and — '

Ivan suddenly found his voice. 'How exactly *do* you elope?'

Amanda spun towards him. 'Are you actually considering this?'

'Yes, I am. I'm as sick of all this carry-on as you are. Sicker, even.' Ivan was growing backbone before Jeannie's eyes. 'Think about it, Mandy. We could just run away. Have our day, our way.'

'You're a poet and you didn't know it.' Amanda started to giggle.

Jeannie tried not to react as they exchanged a too-long kiss in front of her. Once they'd prised themselves apart, they peppered her with questions. She told them everything she knew. There were dozens of how-to-elope websites and companies that arranged it all for you. You picked a location, as exotic as you liked, filled out forms and it went from there.

Amanda's tears had disappeared. 'We'd be the talk of the town, wouldn't we?' She was asking herself the question, not Ivan and Jeannie. 'Imagine what everyone would say! It's like something from Hollywood! And we could throw a huge party when we got back, couldn't we, darling? I could wear my dress again! Have everything exactly the way I wanted! Our own party. Not Kate's.'

Jeannie knew then she'd heard and said enough. She was just leaving the room to start her cleaning when Amanda called after her.

'Could you be a little more careful with the mirror in the bedroom, by the way? It was streaky last week.'

*

For the next few weeks, Jeannie didn't see either sister. Kate was travelling for work. Amanda was spending every morning at the gym. Busy with her studies and a steady stream of new clients, Jeannie was torn between wanting to hear the latest and glad to have the houses to herself to get the cleaning done.

A month to the day since the encounter with Amanda and Ivan, Jeannie let herself into the South Yarra apartment. She noticed immediately that something was different. It was as tidy as she'd left it the previous week. The bed was still made. The bathroom was spotless. The kitchen immaculate. The only signs of life were in the bedroom. The closet doors were open, half the clothes gone. Amanda's expensive cosmetics were missing too.

There was no note. No pay packet, either. It was as if Amanda had just upped and gone.

Upped and gone and . . . ?

Had she? Had they?

As Jeannie stood there, the phone rang. The answering machine clicked into action. Amanda's voice played and then the caller spoke. Shouted, in fact. Jeannie guessed within seconds that it was Amanda's father.

'Amanda, you are in big trouble, young lady! Your mother is hysterical. Kate won't answer her phone. How on earth could you do this? Cancelling all the arrangements at the last minute! Posting us each a wedding photo like that, as if eloping is fine! It's not fine! How do you think Kate will feel, having her wedding ruined like this? Call me as soon as you get this.' The phone was slammed down.

The answering machine was still flashing. Jeannie couldn't stop herself. She pressed the play button. Six older messages poured out, all from Amanda's mother, ranging from tearful to furious to hysterical, all repeating the same themes of horror at the elopement.

It was uncomfortable listening, for too many reasons. Jeannie got to work, doing the little there was to be done as quickly as she could. As she shut the door, she had a feeling she wouldn't be back there again.

She was at Kate's before nine the following day. Her garden looked beautiful in the warm morning sunshine, the flowers swaying in the breeze, sending out a welcoming fragrance. Jeannie knocked, waited a moment, then let herself in. She'd barely slept the night before, thinking about the two sisters, about their mother, hoping Kate wouldn't be too upset today. Maybe she would even be glad. It would take some untangling of arrangements, but perhaps now she and Sam could have exactly the wedding day they wanted.

Jeannie saw the note immediately. It was propped in the middle of the kitchen table, with her pay envelope alongside.

Dear Jeannie,
Sam and I have been away since you last cleaned and we won't be back for another fortnight, so please take a holiday on us. The reason?
We've eloped.

I'm sure it must seem drastic, but it felt exactly right to us. You don't know how much you helped me make this decision, Jeannie, listening to me each week and being so calm and understanding. I kept thinking of something you said to me and you were so right. It was all getting taken away from us and turning into someone else's day. We finally realised it was up to us to make it ours again and this seemed the only – the best – way to do it.

I know from what you said that day that you'll under-stand. I just hope Mum and Dad and Amanda will too . . .

Thank you again, Jeannie, for everything.

Kate and Sam xxx

Jeannie read the note again. Amanda's news yesterday had surprised her, but not touched her. This was different. This she understood. It was a happy, nervous, excited note. A grateful note too.

But all Jeannie could feel was guilt. The last thing she deserved was Kate's gratitude. Because those wise words that Kate had found so helpful hadn't been her words, had they? Jeannie had heard them from someone else, someone very close to her, not in person, but in a phone call, more than four months earlier.

And how had she reacted that time? Had she listened calmly? With understanding?

No. Far from it. She'd lost her temper. Accused the speaker of being selfish, after all that Jeannie had done for her. Cried and shouted and eventually hung up. She'd reacted so badly, been so angry and so hurt that since that day there had been only silence between them, despite the fact they lived less than twenty minutes apart, in the same city.

Her ex-boyfriend Richard had been with her when the phone call came. He'd done his best to act as a go-between. 'Jeannie, I know it's upsetting, and of course you feel hurt, but try and see it from her point of view, can't you?'

She couldn't. She hadn't wanted to. So she told Richard she didn't want to see him again either.

In the weeks that followed, she'd thrown herself into her studies, taken on the cleaning jobs, done all she could to wear herself out so she didn't have to think about either of them.

But it hadn't worked. She'd still thought about them both every day. Watching the battles between Amanda and Kate and their mother, she'd pictured herself in their place. It had been easy to do. Because she had been there herself, in almost that same situation, hadn't she?

Jeannie read Kate's note again. She thought of Kate's joy in her wedding being whittled away by everyone else's expectations. She even felt sympathy for Amanda, and the sisters' mother, for not getting what they wanted either.

What on earth happened to some women at wedding times? Jeannie knew the answer. All sense and reason deserted them. She knew because it had happened to her. It had taken long lonely weeks of thinking to let her see the obvious. She'd been the one at fault.

The solution was even more obvious now. She had to be the one to fix things.

She hesitated for just one moment before taking out her mobile phone and making the first call. As she heard his voice on the answering machine, the measured words she'd planned disappeared. She spoke from the heart instead. 'Richard, it's me. It's Jeannie.' She paused, then forged ahead. 'I'm so sorry for everything. I miss you, every day. If it's not too late, if you'd still like to, would you call me back sometime?'

She needed to take a breath before making the second call. The harder call. She was midway through the number when she changed her mind again. It suddenly didn't seem right to phone when she could be there, in person, in less than fifteen minutes on her bike.

Leaving her cleaning gear behind, she hurried to the front door. Nervous now, she stopped in front of Kate's hall mirror to check her appearance.

An anxious-looking 55-year-old woman looked back at her, in her cleaning outfit of T-shirt and jeans. A stubborn, stupid 55-year-old woman who'd caused her own 25-year-old daughter as much drama and distress as Amanda had caused Kate, as the girls' mother had caused them both.

It seemed so obvious now. Yet for weeks, months even, Jeannie had refused to listen to what her daughter Sarah had been trying to tell her. She'd tried to take over from the first night, when Sarah and Luke told her they'd decided to get married. Not just tried, she *had* taken over, making plans, deciding on arrangements, ignoring Sarah's wishes, Luke's concerns, turning their day – Sarah's day – into her day.

She'd had enough time over the past lonely months to reflect on it. The truth had dawned slowly and painfully, complicated and layered. Had she seen Sarah's wedding day as a chance to make up for the things her daughter had missed out on when she was growing up, with Sarah's father long out of the picture? Yes, that was part of it. She'd also wanted to show off. Not just her happy, well-adjusted, clever daughter, but herself as well. She'd wanted – needed – to prove to her family, her big, judgmental, conservative family, that while she'd made different choices to them over the years, gone down alternative routes, raising Sarah as a single mother, moving from job to job and state to state, even doing something as crazy as throwing in a good job to go back to university at her age – she could still give her only daughter a big, traditional wedding, couldn't she?

A kind of fever had possessed her. Wedding fever. She'd become blind to anyone's suggestions but her own. She'd ignored her daughter's wish to wear a vintage silk dress and taken her to froth- and frill-filled wedding shops instead. She'd ignored Sarah and Luke's idea of a beachside ceremony and insisted on a big wedding in their hometown. She'd become the wedding planner and the mother-of-the-bride from hell.

Sarah had tried to call a halt to it from the start. Jeannie saw that now. So many times she'd started sentences with phrases like, 'Mum, I don't want to hurt your feelings, but . . .' 'Mum,

I agree that would look nice, but it's not what Luke and I want . . .' 'Yes, Mum, it would be great to have everyone in the family there, but it's not really our style . . .'

She'd heard, but she'd chosen not to listen. She'd wanted the wedding day *she'd* never had, the family approval she'd always sought, the opportunity to show off with the best of them. So she'd hijacked her own – her only – daughter's wedding.

Until, two days before it was due to take place, her daughter hijacked it back. Sarah did the one thing she could do to stop it happening.

She'd eloped.

Just like that, she and Luke crept out of the house like two teenagers, caught a plane to Brisbane, met the marriage celebrant they'd secretly organised a month earlier and got married on a beach, with two witnesses and a glorious sunset behind them.

Sarah had rung Jeannie to tell her. It was the worst phone call Jeannie had ever taken. Tears, anger, long silences, pleas for understanding on both sides. Jeannie had been overcome with a rush of hurt and humiliation. Her only daughter hadn't wanted her own mother at her wedding.

She wouldn't listen to Sarah's attempts to explain, not that day on the phone and not since. She had returned any letters Sarah had sent. Not opened any emails.

She had sulked, there was no other word for it. A woman of her age, behaving like a child. Sarah's elopement hadn't been a slap in the face, she realised now. It had been a wake-up call: Sarah's only way of showing that she was now an adult, that she could and needed to make her own decisions. That it was time for Jeannie to let go.

And how had she repaid her? With months of silence.

As Jeannie cycled through the Melbourne streets now, she could feel the tears welling. She hadn't let herself cry since the day of the phone call, hanging on to the hurt and anger instead. She didn't try to stop the tears now. Not until she had arrived at the door to Sarah and Luke's apartment building. She got off the bike, breathed slowly, wiped her eyes and prayed that luck would be on her side, that Sarah, an architect, still worked from home on Tuesdays.

She pressed the intercom button, realising she was holding her breath. Thirty long seconds passed before she heard a voice. Her daughter's voice, turned tinny by the speaker.

'Hello?'

Jeannie's heart started to beat faster just hearing it. She sounded busy. Distracted. Jeannie hesitated for one second, and then spoke.

'Sarah?'

'*Mum?* Mum, is that you?'

Jeannie nodded, then realised how silly that was. Sarah couldn't see her. 'I'm downstairs. I'm —' Sorry. Heartbroken. Ashamed. All of those things. 'I'm downstairs,' she said again.

There was no answer. No buzz of the front door being

opened for her. No voice in reply. Jeannie stood, staring at the intercom, willing her daughter's voice to sound from it again.

It stayed quiet.

Jeannie couldn't blame her. How could she? Who did Jeannie think she was, turning up, expecting instant forgiveness after the way she'd behaved?

She was turning to unlock her bike, to cycle away again, when she heard something.

It was footsteps. A person in a hurry, their feet pounding down the staircase inside, getting closer and closer.

The door flew open. It wasn't just a person. It was her daughter, her Sarah, dressed only in a towel, obviously just out of the shower, her hair streaming wet, her eyes filled with tears.

'Oh, *Mum!*'

That was all Jeannie managed to see and hear, before she felt the beautiful, familiar rush of her daughter flying back into her arms.

Odd One Out

1

Though Sylvie Devereaux didn't realise it at the time, her life began to change at exactly five minutes past seven on the evening of her sister Vanessa's second wedding.

The instigator was her Great-Aunt Mill. 'Mill-as-in-short-for-Millicent,' as she always introduced herself. Great-Aunt Foot-in-Mouth, the rest of the family privately called her.

It had been a hectic day for the Devereaux family. As the Sydney society pages would report the following morning: *Two artistic dynasties came together yesterday with the union of fashion designer Vanessa Devereaux and actor Jared Rowe. A who's who of the Sydney art scene was in attendance, including the bride's mother, the celebrated artist Fidelma Devereaux, the bride's sister and bridesmaid, jewellery designer Cleo Devereaux, and her brother Sebastian Devereaux, winner of this year's Green Room Award for outstanding achievement in lighting design. Vanessa, a rising star in the Sydney fashion scene, designed her own dress, a daring and colourful interpretation of the classic Grecian shift style . . .* There would be no mention of Sylvie.

The reception was taking place in the city's most talked-about harbourside restaurant. Dinner was served by waiters who looked like models. Rock oysters to begin. Pan-fried sole with truffle shavings and porcini mushrooms on a bed of baby spinach for main course. A concoction of summer berries in an amusement of toffee for dessert.

Sitting one row away from the main bridal table, Sylvie was catching her breath. She'd been on the run all day. Checking details with the celebrant, the photographer, the caterer, the musicians. Fetching the flowers. Returning the flowers when Vanessa wasn't happy with them. Moving furniture in the hotel suite at Vanessa's insistence. Moving it back at the photographer's insistence. Driving to the family home to fetch a handbag her mother had left behind. Stopping on the way at her mother and sisters' studio to collect a necklace Cleo had forgotten. Going back to the studio and the house again for more handbags and necklaces when they changed their minds. Keeping everyone fed and hydrated, dialling room service so many times she was on first-name terms with the receptionist.

She'd had fifteen minutes to race home again, do her own make-up and try to style her short curly hair. One minute to lament her ordinary brown eyes and freckled skin, so different from her sisters' blue-eyed classic features. Five minutes to change into her wedding outfit. A normal outfit, not a bridesmaid's dress. Vanessa had asked Cleo to be bridesmaid, again. 'It's good for both our profiles, Sylvie. You understand,' Vanessa said. Sylvie said that of course she did, and hoped her smile hid her hurt. She'd secretly hoped this time it was her turn. Or that Vanessa would have two bridesmaids. When she tentatively suggested this, Vanessa explained it was more fashionable these days to have one.

In her room, Sylvie thought her outfit looked lovely, a green silk dress and matching jacket, green high-heeled shoes and glass earrings. At only five foot two, she'd learnt to avoid complicated patterns or fussy designs. 'You've come as an elf, how sweet,' was all Cleo said. Her mother was too busy directing the hairdresser to pin up her long hair in a particular way to notice Sylvie's outfit. She just gave her a vague wave and said she looked charming. She'd said the same thing about Sylvie's working clothes of jeans and T-shirt that morning. Vanessa didn't say anything. She was too busy posing for photographs. Sylvie's only hope for a compliment was from her big brother, Sebastian, her closest ally in the family. As a child, Sylvie had secretly thought of him as her separated twin, cheerfully ignoring the seven-year age difference. They were very alike in appearance even now. Unfortunately, his flight from Melbourne had been delayed so many times it looked like the most he'd see of the wedding was the cutting of the cake.

Sebastian finally arrived at the reception at seven p.m. Sylvie's spirits lifted as he came through the garlanded door. Although they'd spoken on the phone now and again, it was the first time they'd seen each other in ten months. He was out of his normal jeans and casual shirts, dressed in a dark-blue suit and a red tie, his unruly hair tamed into a more sober style than usual. Short for a man, only five foot six, he was often mistaken for a mid-twenties student, not the thirty-six-year-old success story he was. 'It's my boyish charm, not my height,' he always said.

Sylvie had heard Vanessa on the phone, unsubtly telling him he needed to dress up for the occasion. 'A lot of my clients will be here, Sebastian. I want to make the right impression. Not like last time.' He'd come straight from a country film set to her first wedding, dirt still on his shoes. She hadn't spoken to him for weeks. 'I can see her point,' he'd said to Sylvie. 'It's my fault the marriage failed. If I'd worn a suit they'd be celebrating their fifth anniversary about now.' When he'd heard the decorative theme of this wedding was water, he'd told Sylvie he was thinking about coming in a wetsuit.

Sylvie was waving to get his attention when she heard her name being called. Shouted, in fact. It was Great-Aunt Mill, across the room at the elderly-members-of-the-family table. In her early seventies, short and plump, she was dressed in a red dress with a wide cream collar. She had pinned her white hair into a lopsided bun, adding a jaunty red bow to the back. The whole effect was unfortunately like a giant jelly cake.

Sylvie excused herself to her neighbour (an old school friend of Vanessa's who'd spent the past hour talking about his stock portfolio) and made her way through the round, beautifully decorated tables. Each blue and white flower arrangement had cost more than Sylvie's dress. She'd barely sat down before Great-Aunt Mill took her hand.

'You're not to worry, little Sylvie.'

'About what, Aunt Mill?'

'About being left on the shelf.'

'But I'm not worried.'

'Of course you are. Any girl would be on a day like today. You're probably thinking, "It's not fair. One of my sisters is long married, the other has been married twice. That's our family's share of weddings all used up." Unless Sebastian surprises us, of course, but they don't tend to marry, his sort of people, do they? They're not allowed to, are they? We all guessed even when he was a young boy, you know. Always putting on those little plays and asking for dance lessons. Is he here yet? I haven't seen him. But it's not him I'm concerned about, it's you. "I've missed out," you're thinking. "I'm going to be single for life."'

'I wasn't, really.'

Mill patted Sylvie's hand. 'It can be hard being the youngest one, I know. My youngest sister, Letitia, that's your other great-aunt, was never happy. Couldn't seem to find her place in the world. You look like her, you know. Small. That same springy hair. Same big smile too. You might be taking after her in life as well. Not that she lived long. Died aged twenty-four, God rest her soul. Measles. Or was it chicken pox? Something spotty anyway.'

'I'm nearly out of my twenties, Mill. I should be okay. And I'm fit as a fiddle.'

'Of course you are. Anyone can see that. You've got your grandfather's farming genes in you. Fine agricultural bloodstock. Strong and sturdy, like a little ox.' Aunt Mill leaned in close enough for Sylvie to get a quick blast of sherry-scented breath. 'Which is why I have a proposition for you.'

'To sell me as breeding stock?'

Aunt Mill gave a burst of laughter. 'How funny. Now, you've been working around Sydney as a pimp for the past few years, your mother tells me.'

'A temp, Mill.'

'A tip? What about?'

'Temp. I'm a temp, Mill. It's short for temporary secretary.'

'Nothing to be ashamed about. It can't be easy to find permanent work these days. And not everyone gets given a special talent like your mother did. And your sisters. And your brother. Your father too, though I probably shouldn't mention him on a happy day like today. He's not here, I suppose? No, of course he isn't. As I was saying, the rest of us are the worker bees. I was a housekeeper all my life, as you know, and it never did me any harm. Where is it you said you're working?'

Sylvie was tempted to say a side street in Kings Cross. 'I'm working back at the studio again, with Mum and Vanessa and Cleo. Doing their admin.' They'd called her in a panic six months previously, when their regular PA walked out in a huff on the eve of an exhibition opening. Sylvie had been there since. Apart from answering the phone, typing letters, sending orders, updating databases and doing filing, she also ran errands, booked restaurants, sent flowers and kept an eye on their supplies of herbal tea, spring water, rice cakes, pecans, blueberries, vitamin tablets and eye gel.

'A family affair. Oh, good, so you've had some experience.'

'Of what?'

'Working for family.'

The squeal of the microphone interrupted. The speeches were due to start. Sylvie was about to whisper to Mill that she might like to turn her chair around when the old woman put her hand on her arm and gave it a surprisingly tight squeeze. 'I've been watching you all day. Busy as a bee. Grace under pressure. I do believe you're the perfect candidate.'

'I am? For what?'

The best man clinked his glass. The room fell silent. All eyes were turned towards the top table. Which meant that all ninety-five people in the room, including Sylvie's mother, her mother's boyfriend, her three siblings, two brothers-in-law, five well-known Sydney artists, two critics, three gallery owners and sixty members of the Devereaux family's social circle not only clearly heard but also saw Great-Aunt Mill lean over and shout her idea.

'I'm offering you a job as my companion, Sylvie. We can be two old maids together.'

2

'So did you accept? It's certainly the offer of a lifetime.'

'I gracefully declined but I said you'd be more than happy to take up the position.'

Sebastian laughed. 'Poor Sylvie. You should have seen your face.'

'I didn't need to see it. I could feel it. And I could see everyone else's faces. Hear them laughing.'

'Not all of them.'

'Don't try and gloss over it, Seb. Everyone heard. Everyone in the room. Everyone in Sydney.'

'Only the inner suburbs. Spin, Sylvie.'

She obeyed, executing a graceful turn. Sebastian had appeared out of nowhere onto the dance floor one song previously, rescuing her from the overly sweaty hands of her dinner partner. 'Excuse me cutting in. I haven't seen my little sister all night.'

'So where is this pad of yours and Mill's?'

'Mum didn't tell you? Mill's old boss Vincent left her his house, contents and all. It's a two-storey terrace in Surry Hills. She moved in last month.'

Sebastian gave a low whistle. 'That's what I call being a housekeeper. Get it, Sylvie? Housekeeper, keeper of the house?'

'Got it, Seb.'

Sylvie had only met Vincent once, when Great-Aunt Mill brought him to a family gathering. A beetle-browed, slightly stooped man, he had glowered at them all for an hour and then left in a taxi. He'd once been a well-known musician and composer, apparently. Jazz, Sylvie thought. Or was it blues? He'd died of a heart attack several months earlier. Mill had rung and told the family about his death, and her inheritance, sounding surprisingly chipper, Fidelma reported. 'No wonder,' Vanessa had said sniffily. 'Those terrace houses are worth a fortune. I'd be sounding quite chipper myself.'

'She must have been more than his cook and cleaner all those years,' Cleo had said, disgusted. 'I think it's appalling.'

'At least you got your embarrassing Mill moment out of the way early,' Sebastian said as they finished a complicated move. 'Now you can relax. Enjoy yourself.'

'Knowing everyone thinks I'm an old maid?'

'They heard your batty old relative ask you a batty old question. They didn't see you fall on your knees in gratitude and accept. *That* would have been truly embarrassing. For me, at least. Not to mention the rest of your family.'

Their next turn around the dance floor gave Sylvie the perfect view of the rest of her family. Her mother was holding court at the head table. Fidelma had switched seamlessly from her earlier modest mother-of-the-bride role back to Fidelma Devereaux the famous artist, all dramatic gestures and fluttering eyelashes. Sylvie could almost hear her trying to find the exact word to describe a colour or idea she hoped to express in her work. Beside Fidelma was her latest boyfriend, Ray, a not-so-successful artist, poised like a gun dog, ready as always to fetch Fidelma a drink, a cigarette or a more comfortable chair.

Vanessa and her new husband were waltzing cheek-to-cheek five couples away. Vanessa's azure blue dress caught the light, with its shimmers, sparkles and elegant lines. Her long blonde hair was a beautiful contrast against it. The photographer was trailing behind them, taking action shots.

Her other sister Cleo and her lawyer husband were standing by the bar. Cleo had her hand extended, showing a dramatic ring to its greatest advantage. She was her own best advertisement, her handcrafted silver jewellery adorning her fingers, wrist and neck, several glittering hairpins in her blonde curls. Sylvie had already heard her make two appointments to discuss future orders.

'Dip, Sylvie.'

She dipped. Sebastian had taught her to dance when she was a child, just a few months before he and their father left the family home and moved to Melbourne. He'd made a point of giving her refresher lessons every year when he came to Sydney to stay, hearing all her news at the same time. There was plenty to catch up on today. He'd had the busiest year of his career, designing the lighting for three films and two plays. Even this trip was a brief one. He was going back to Melbourne early the next day.

The music changed from the fast salsa beat to a waltz. 'Here's our chance,' he said. 'Music to talk by. Before we start, Dad says hello, by the way.'

'Does he?'

'Don't be like that.'

'Like what?'

'You've gone stiff as a board. Not good for our dancing style.'

'Please say hello back to him.'

'Such warmth and enthusiasm.'

'It's hard to think of anything else to say to him.' Sylvie didn't understand these new attempts by Sebastian to pass on messages from their long-estranged father. She actually wondered whether they were coming from their father at all. 'It's different for us, Seb. Harder.'

'Of course it is. You poor things. I forget.'

'Don't be cross.'

'I'm not cross. Really. Let's talk about you instead. I want a full update.'

'You first. I haven't seen you in months.'

'In a nutshell? Work, great. House, great. Social life, great. Your turn.'

'Social life great? You've met someone?'

'I'm not here to talk about me.'

'You have! Who is he? Where?'

'Someone. In Melbourne.'

'You can't leave it at that.'

'I'm older than you. I can do as I please. Your turn. Start with work. Please tell me you're not still at Union Street.' It was the family's shorthand name for the studio, a converted warehouse in the east inner city. Fidelma, Vanessa and Cleo had recently started calling it Avalon. The name had come to Fidelma in a dream.

'I'm still at Union Street.'

'You promised me you were going to leave. Work anywhere but there.'

'I did leave. Then I came back.' She read his expression. 'I had to, Seb. They needed me. Mum rang me in an absolute panic.'

'Which is why you're back living at home too?'

Back in the family house at Rushcutters Bay, back in her old bedroom. She was even sleeping in her old bed.

'I know I said I'd never go back, but my flatmate was moving to Brisbane and when Mum rang . . .'

'And said that it was all over between her and Ray yet again and she couldn't bear another night in the house on her own, you couldn't say no?'

'It wasn't like that.' It had been exactly like that.

'And friends? Or have you cast them out of your life as well?'

'I've plenty of friends,' she said, stung. It was true. She had friends from the arts course she'd started at Sydney University as a nineteen-year-old, ten years ago now. People she'd met in student jobs in wine bars and coffee shops. Other temps from the executive agency she'd been with for six years. Everyone was so busy these days, though, getting married or starting to have babies. Settling down. She was the only single one among her group these days.

'So your love life is hectic and fulfilling too?'

She was glad the dance steps meant she could avoid eye contact for a moment. Her love life was like the Sahara. 'Nothing since David.'

'Evil David? That was months ago. No one since? Have you been out with anyone? Asked friends to set you up? Advertised your wares?'

'No, no, no and no. And if I ever asked you those questions you'd tell me to mind my own business.'

'True. Spin.' They spun. 'Have you had a break since I saw you last? One of those old-fashioned things called a holiday?'

'No,' she said simply.

'Sylvie, go to the kitchen and get two spoons, would you?'

'Why?'

'I've arrived in the nick of time. Things are worse for you

than I thought. We're going to dig you a tunnel out of here, through the dance floor. I'm thinking *The Great Escape*. Or am I thinking *Chicken Run*? Whichever it is, you need freedom. A new start. Liberty and justice.'

'You're quoting from a play now, aren't you?'

He grinned. 'Just the liberty and justice line, yes. I blame myself. I've neglected you this year.'

'You haven't. And I don't need rescuing. I like being busy.'

'You've gone beyond busy. I can see it just looking at you. You've got "I am stressed" written in block letters on your forehead.'

She rubbed at her forehead without thinking. 'We've had a lot on this year. Three exhibitions. Cleo's new line of jewellery. Vanessa's export orders.'

'So presumably they haven't had holidays either?'

Fidelma had been away to her house on the coast most weekends the past year. Cleo had been to Paris twice. Vanessa had been to Vietnam and Hong Kong. In search of inspiration, they'd said each time.

'You don't have to answer, I can see it on your face,' he said. 'And you kept the home fires burning each time? The office lights ablaze?'

'There was a lot to do, Seb. And I wanted to do it properly.'

'And are they paying you properly?'

'As much as they can. Most of the profits go straight back into the business.'

'Straight back into their holiday funds, you mean. Sylvie, why do you keep falling for this? Any time you try to get away, Mum reels you back in. As for Heckle and Jeckle —'

She secretly loved it when Sebastian called Vanessa and Cleo by their childhood nicknames. Especially when he did it to their faces.

He wasn't laughing. 'I'm serious, Sylvie. They're not good to you or for you. You have to get away from them.' He led her skilfully in a sudden complicated dance move. 'I couldn't do it when you were a kid, but I can do it now. I'm airlifting you out of here. Kidnapping you. You're coming to live in Melbourne with me.'

'Really? Great. Let me go and get my bag.'

'It's not a joke. I mean it.'

'You're mad. I can't move to Melbourne, Seb. I've got work here. A life here.'

'What life? Back living at home, at Mum's beck and call? And you haven't got work, you've got penal servitude.'

'I'm fine.'

'You're not fine. I've been watching you since I got here. You've got that expression you used to have when you were little. This one.' He demonstrated it. A worried, anxious expression.

He had it exactly right. It was like looking in a mirror. She forced a smile. 'It's a nice idea —'

'A nice idea?'

'A really nice idea. But I can't just up and leave. Mum needs me here.'

'Sylvie, can I be blunt? Ever hear that story "Cinderella"? The one about the little servant girl and her cruel family? You're turning into her.'

'I'm not. I don't sit by the fire.' She pointed her toes. 'And I don't have glass slippers.'

'They treat you just as badly. Mum doesn't mean to, I know. She's self-centred, but she's not malicious. Heckle and Jeckle are different. I can imagine them today – "Fetch this, do that". Am I right?'

She knew her face gave her away. 'Today was an unusual day.'

'Why, because they noticed you? I've heard them talk to you like that whether it's a wedding or not. They're squashing you, Sylvie. They did it when you were little and they're doing it now. You need to get away from them. Why are you putting up with it?'

'I told you, I like being busy.'

'There's busy and there's being a mouse on a wheel. I'm worried about you.'

'Don't be.'

'Always have, always will. I'm serious about Melbourne, Sylvie. I'm also being selfish. I'm going away on a three-week shoot next month and I want a house-sitter. Someone to water my plants, keep my neighbours at bay. The person I'd lined up cancelled on me this week. I was about to advertise but now there's no need. You'd be perfect. And you'd be doing me a huge favour.'

'You're making that up.'

'I'm not making it up. I can show you the wording for the ad.'

'But I can't leave everyone here in the lurch.'

'What lurch? Vanessa's on honeymoon for the next month. Mum's going to her beach house to paint.' He refused to call it 'the retreat', as Fidelma did. 'Cleo's going on holiday as well, she told me. To Byron, I think. Or Palm Beach. Somewhere glamorous, anyway.'

'She is?' Cleo hadn't mentioned anything to Sylvie about a holiday. 'It'll be a good time to catch up while everyone's away, then,' she said, finding a bright voice. 'I've loads of filing to do. A new database to set up.'

'Can I ask you a direct question?'

'Your others weren't direct?'

He ignored her sarcasm. 'Are you happy, Sylvie? At work? At home? With life?'

'Deliriously.' To her dismay she felt a prickle of tears in her eyes. She blinked them away. 'It's the champagne. I'm fine. I'm absolutely fine.'

'It's not the champagne.' He drew her to the side of the dance floor and found her a chair. 'You used to say the same thing to me when you were little, you know, when Mum and Dad were screaming at each other. "I'm fine. Absolutely fine." You'd copied it from a British TV show. *Upstairs, Downstairs* or something.'

He was right, she had. She managed a smile. 'Well, I am

fine. I'm absolutely fine.' She said it in a perfect cut-glass Eng-lish accent.

He pulled up a chair beside her. 'I didn't believe you then and I don't now. What is it? What's happened?'

The combination of too much champagne, the exhaus-tion of the past few days and the concern on her brother's face prompted the truth. 'Something silly. I might have got it wrong, though. Misheard it.'

'Misheard what?'

'Mum.'

'Tell me.'

Sylvie knew she hadn't misheard it. Her mother had been pointing out her family to a guest at the wedding. A dealer, Sylvie thought. Someone high up in the art world, at least. Fidelma had pointed out Cleo and Vanessa, the beautiful bride. She'd said that Sebastian was on his way from Melbourne. 'You've heard of him, of course?' 'Of course,' the man had said. Fidelma had listed all their achievements, talked about the joys of an artistic household, of their dramatic sensibil-ity as a family. Sylvie had heard most of it many times in interviews. 'And your other daughter?' the man had asked. 'You've three, haven't you?'

Sylvie hesitated before finishing. 'And Mum said to him, "Oh, yes, there's Sylvie, my youngest. But she doesn't really do anything."'

'I'll kill her,' Sebastian said.

'It's true, Seb. I don't do anything. Nothing lasting.'

'You work harder than anyone I know. You've got a degree. You haven't been out of work since you left uni. The only difference is you're not a bloody show pony about it.'

Sylvie was surprised at how angry he seemed. 'She's got a point. So do you. I am Cinderella. Look at our family, Seb. Artist, fashion designer, jeweller, lighting genius, secretary. Can you pick the odd one out?'

'You're not just a secretary and you know it. What was the name of that high-flying temp agency you used to work for? The one that sounded like a brothel?'

'Executive Stress Relief.' It was an agency specialising in emergency high-level secretarial support, for everyone from top business people to government ministers. Sylvie had been their employee of the year for the past four years. Her boss, Jill, had told her there was a position waiting back with them whenever she wanted.

'You've got them as a safety net, haven't you? If you were to leave Union Street?'

'Yes, but I'm not looking for a safety net.'

'No, what you need is an escape chute.' He was thoughtful for a moment. 'You remember when you were little, and I used to do those treasure hunts for you? With the dares?'

'Of course. You made me eat a worm once, do you remember?'

'I didn't make you. You misread the clue.'

Sylvie had loved those treasure hunts, Sebastian's birthday presents to her from the time she was eight until she turned fourteen. He'd devised a series of clues based on her favourite books. They'd taken her days to solve sometimes. Each one had led to a challenge or special treat of some sort. One year, she found herself up on the roof of the house, building a cubby from a bed sheet and a fold-up chair. Another year, he dared her to spend the night in the garden of their suburb's allegedly haunted house. She lasted all night, to Sebastian's amazement.

'I hereby resurrect the days of the treasure hunts. Sylvie Devereaux, I dare you to come to Melbourne.'

Sylvie laughed. 'Good one. You forgot the clues, though. And I'm not a kid any more.'

'Don't change the subject. Come on. I dare you. Even for a few weeks. Let's call it a trial run. A holiday. An escape.'

'Let's call it madness. I've got a job here.'

'That's all that's stopping you?'

'Yes, but —'

'Stay here.'

She watched as he went to their mother, then Vanessa, then Cleo. All three listened, nodded. They were soon smiling, laughing even. They adored Sebastian. Everyone did. He was back within five minutes. 'It's settled. You're coming to Melbourne.'

'Really? Just like that? And what did Mum say?'

'Do you want the truth?'

Sylvie nodded.

'She didn't bat an eyelid. I said, "Sylvie's worried about

leaving work behind," and she said, "Oh, we'll get someone else from an agency. There's not much to it." '

The words felt like a punch. 'What about being in the house on her own?'

'Ray was doing the Revolting Tickling Thing on the back of her neck while she was talking.' Sebastian had dubbed it that the last time he was home. 'So it looks like you're off the hook there as well.'

'And Vanessa and Cleo?'

'Thought it was a great idea. Just what you needed, they said.'

It was like being patronised, hit and encouraged, all at once. She'd half-hoped her sisters would listen with alarm to Sebastian's suggestion, come across and say, 'But, Sylvie, what will we do without you?' She looked over. They were involved in animated conversations with their friends, as if Sebastian's suggestion had had no impact. She'd worked long days, nights and weekends for them. She thought she'd been making a dif-ference, helping them, keeping the studio running.

She turned in time to see her mother move gracefully to the open window and stand within its frame, the curves of the Opera House a striking backdrop to her floaty dress and tum-ble of hair. The setting was no accident, Sylvie knew. Fidelma had a knack of posing for maximum visual impact. Ray joined her and began the Revolting Tickling Thing again. Sebastian was right, their on-again off-again relationship was clearly back on. Which meant Ray would soon be back living in the house, taking over the kitchen, prefacing all his sentences with 'Fidelma's asked me to ask you . . .'

Two tables away, Great-Aunt Mill was talking loudly. 'I still don't know why everyone laughed,' she was saying. 'I was quite serious about her being my companion. I think we'd be very happy together.'

Sebastian was watching Sylvie's face closely. 'Well?'

She stood up. 'Ready when you are,' she said.

3

For the third time since Sebastian had left for his film shoot that morning, Sylvie took herself on a tour of his Melbourne apartment.

It was on the second floor of a converted red-brick mansion in South Yarra, two streets from the Botanic Gardens. He'd moved in eight months before, after years of flat-shares with other theatre people around Melbourne. The apartment was like a stage set itself, with high ceilings, bay windows, polished wooden floorboards and ornate ceiling roses.

'If anyone wanted to do *This is Your Life* on me, it's all here,' he'd said as he showed Sylvie around. The sofa was from an Oscar Wilde play he'd worked on. The chandelier from a modern Shakespeare. Paintings from an opera set. A mirror from a music video. The walls in the entrance hall were covered in framed photos of his friends and family. There was a futon in one bedroom, an elaborate carved sleigh-type bed in the other, rich red rugs on the floor of both. The whole effect was a cross between a flea market, an antiques store and backstage at a theatre. She loved it.

She hadn't moved down immediately after the wedding. Sebastian had asked for a week to get himself packed and organised for the film shoot. She'd used the time in Sydney to organise the already organised office at Union Street and leave notes for any incoming temp. She'd tidied up her already tidy bedroom in the family home. She met friends for fare-well drinks and dinner. She had lunch with Jill, the boss of Executive Stress Relief, who made a point of taking all her Melbourne contact details. She was hoping to be there in the next few weeks and wanted to meet up again.

'I can actually picture you living in Melbourne,' she'd said to Sylvie. 'Are you planning on staying long?'

'A few weeks initially. With an eye to the long term.' It felt brave saying that. 'I'll get in touch with temp agencies and real estate agents as soon as I get there.'

Jill was impressed. 'You're certainly hitting the ground running.'

'That's the plan,' Sylvie said, hoping Jill couldn't see her fingers were crossed under the table.

Vanessa, Cleo and her mother had all left Sydney the day after the wedding. Vanessa left a message on the machine wishing Sylvie a safe trip and asking her to make sure the trade-fair orders had been dispatched. Cleo left a note saying have fun and asking her to collect her dry-cleaning before she went. Her mother took her out for a farewell coffee and talked the entire time about how wonderful it was to have Ray back in her life.

The only person in Sylvie's family who'd seemed interested in her trip to Melbourne was Great-Aunt Mill. She'd left messages on the office answering machine all week, either before Sylvie got in or late at night.

'I hear you're popping down to Melbourne for a little holiday with Sebastian, Sylvie. What a lovely idea. We'll be busy when you get back – Vincent left boxes and boxes of material to sort through – so I'm glad you'll be fresh.'

'Sylvie, I've found a gardener, so that's the outside of the house taken care of, while you and I make a start on the inside. Vincent wasn't much of a gardener, I'm afraid. Though he did like trees.'

'I was going to organise the painters for your room but you might like to choose the colours yourself, Sylvie. It's blue at the moment. Such a lovely aspect from that room. A view right over the city. There's a fig tree too. I've made delicious jam from it over the years. Vincent's favourite.'

'You're off tomorrow, I believe? Safe trip. Will you be warm enough there? Vincent always hated Melbourne. Far too cold for him. I've got Sebastian's number so I'll be in touch if I need to.'

She'd ended each call with the same message: 'No need to ring back.'

'You *do* need to ring her back. You have to be straight with her,' Sebastian said after she told him about the calls. 'Just ring her and say, "Thanks again for the kind offer, but I'm not moving in with you, you crazy old coot."'

'She's not a crazy old coot.'

'She's the queen of crazy old coots.'

'She's just lonely. She must be missing Vincent a lot. And I don't want to hurt her feelings.'

Sylvie had always felt a bit sorry for Mill. She often seemed to be either lost in the crowd or ignored at family occasions, even though she was always the first to respond to any invitation. Fidelma was quite vague about who she actually was. Her late grandmother's sister, she finally remembered. Or was it cousin? They all called her Great-Aunt for convenience. Until she'd inherited Vincent's Surry Hills home, she'd lived in a small flat in Newtown, travelling across town for nearly forty years to work as his cook and cleaner, six days a week. She always arrived at family gatherings with several large plastic containers filled with her homemade biscuits, buns and exquisitely iced cakes.

Sylvie called her back and left a polite message on her machine. 'Thanks for your calls, Mill. I'm not sure how long I'll be in Melbourne but I'll be in touch as soon as I know a bit more about my future plans.'

What future plans? she wondered as she walked through Sebastian's apartment again, a nervous feeling in her stomach. All her pre-trip bravado seemed to have evaporated, now she was here. It wasn't that she was worried about being in Melbourne on her own. She knew it reasonably well, having been down with Fidelma for several exhibition openings over the years. She was scared of something else. The reality of it not meeting the fantasy she'd built in her head all her life.

Melbourne had been her Utopia. Whenever things were difficult at home with her mother or sisters after the divorce, as a child and later as a teenager, she'd imagined herself living in Melbourne with Sebastian and her father. Sebastian had sent her postcards from there nearly every week in the early years. They had taken up almost a wall of her bedroom. She built whole stories around the photographs. That green tram was the one she and Sebastian would catch to school. The long street – Swanston Street – was where they would go walking on Sundays, Sebastian on one side of her, her father on the other. She imagined boat trips together on the Yarra in winter, picnics on the beach at St Kilda in summer. They'd go to see plays at the Arts Centre. Football matches at the MCG. She would barrack for Essendon, she decided. She was the only girl in her class at school who knew all the Australian Rules football teams. She kept it to herself, though. She'd never told anyone about her secret Melbourne life. Not even Sebastian.

He had given her a soft and welcoming landing on this trip. He'd met her at Tullamarine airport, holding up a sign, wearing a peaked cap and guiding her outside to where a limousine was waiting. 'It's not every day Cinderella comes to stay,' he said. He admitted later that the owner of the car was a friend of his and had lent it as a favour.

They had two days together before he left. He took her on a guided tour of the Botanic Gardens and treated her to coffee and cake in the café inside the gates. The trees were wearing the slightest tinge of autumn red and gold. They visited the nearby streets and shops in South Yarra, Richmond and Prahran. She met friends of his in the local milk bar, laundry, Greek restaurant, Thai restaurant and Japanese noodle bar.

He made a special point of taking her to a small bookshop three streets from his house. The owner, a smiling, grey-haired Scottish man in his early forties, looked up with pleasure as they came in.

'Here she is, Don,' Sebastian said, putting his arm around Sylvie. 'Sylvie, Donald. Donald, my little sister Sylvie. She's my representative on earth while I'm away so please treat her with the respect and adoration you would normally show me.'

'Welcome, Sylvie,' Donald said, getting into the spirit, kissing her hand gallantly. 'Come and see us any time. Any sister of Sebastian's is, let me think, what's that saying —' he paused, 'hopefully less trouble than he is.'

'You'll miss me while I'm gone,' Sebastian said. He glanced around the shop. 'Is Max here?'

'Day off, Seb, sorry. I'll tell him you dropped in.'

As Donald turned to serve a customer, Sebastian spoke quietly to Sylvie. 'I really want you to meet Max. He's a very good friend of mine. I've asked him to keep an eye on you as well.'

Something in Sebastian's tone caught Sylvie's attention. A very good friend? As in more than a friend? As in the someone Sebastian had met recently? Her brother had always been good at getting personal details out of her, and keeping his own life secret. She had a hunch he'd just given away more than he realised.

'It'll be great to meet him,' she said.

At a farewell dinner the evening before, Sebastian had taken her to a small Italian restaurant a few blocks from his apartment. The handwritten menu had run to ten pages. When she'd asked him to order for her, he was appalled. 'You don't know about Italian food?'

'Of course I do. But you're the expert.'

'Then you have to become one too. Italian food's one of the great pleasures of life, Sylvie.'

'I thought you told me dancing was.'

'Food – any kind of food, not only Italian – dancing, love and sleep. That's all anyone needs to be happy.'

Sylvie did like food and liked cooking too. She'd just got out of practice, living at home. As she explained to Sebastian, Fidelma had developed food allergies recently.

He raised an eyebrow. 'That would be from the same family of allergies that stopped you having real pets when you were little?'

Sylvie had forgotten what a good memory Sebastian had. As

148

a seven-year-old, she'd invented an imaginary kitten, one that wouldn't give her mother allergies. She called it Silky, after the fairy in her favourite Enid Blyton books. Silky miraculously had kittens herself a few weeks later. Sylvie named them after her other favourite book characters. At one stage there were fifteen imaginary kittens living in her bedroom.

'Why do you hate Mum so much, Seb?' she asked now.

'I don't hate her. I actually enjoy her hugely. What I hate is how she controls you.'

'She doesn't.'

'No, of course she doesn't. And if she did, she doesn't any more because I have whisked you from under her sweet little allergic nose. So tell me, what were the last three meals you cooked?'

'For Mum and me?'

'For anyone.'

Sylvie thought back. 'Pasta with tomato sauce. Vegetable soup. Tofu and steamed vegetables.' Fidelma had been in a vegetarian phase. Six months earlier she had eaten nothing but steamed fish. Before that, only grilled organic meat.

'Not a spice or herb to be found? You are what you eat, Sylvie. No wonder your life has been so dull lately.'

'I told you, Mum's got a particular palate.'

'Sylvie, one more day there and you'd have turned into a blancmange yourself. I am going to drip-feed chilli and fish sauce into you while you sleep. We can work on you internally and externally. Spice up your life in more ways than one.

We can rebuild you. We have the technology.' Sebastian held up his glass. 'To your trial run, Sylvie.'

'To my trial run.'

They clinked glasses.

An hour later, their main courses of homemade tortellini and potato gnocchi finished, she refilled their glasses and lifted hers in another toast. 'Thank you, Sebastian.'

'For what?'

'The wine. The dinner. The escape chute. The house-sitting. Everything.'

'Don't thank me yet. I'm hardly started.'

'What do you mean?'

'Mind your own business.' He called over the waiter then. 'Tiramisu to share, Sylvie? No, we're too old to share. Two servings of tiramisu, Tony, please.'

They ate their dessert, the rich coffee-soaked cake wrapped in thick cream. Their espresso coffees had just arrived when Sebastian shifted in his seat and said in a conversational tone, 'Did I tell you Dad's living in Collingwood these days?'

She had been waiting for Sebastian to mention him. It had been the one subject hanging between them since she arrived. She'd expected Fidelma to say something before she left too and was surprised when she hadn't. Perhaps she felt she didn't need to. Sylvie had heard it all so many times in her life she didn't need refreshing. 'He's a bad man, Sylvie. A lying, manipulative, cruel man.' 'Why would you want to go and visit him? I couldn't bear it if you did, Sylvie. It's enough for me to cope with that he took Sebastian from me.' 'Of course it's no surprise he hasn't sent you a birthday card, Sylvie. When did he ever think of anyone but himself?' Sylvie blinked, dismissing her mother's voice.

'Does he?' she said.

'Not that far from here. I can leave you his phone number if you want it.'

'Seb, I know what you're trying to do. It's too late.'

'Why? He's only in his sixties. He can still walk and talk.'

Sylvie knew that. She'd seen the occasional reference to him in the literary pages of the newspapers, whenever his poems were included in new anthologies. Even so many years on, Fidelma would rage against him if she saw his name or photograph. 'Look at him. Like butter wouldn't melt in his mouth.'

'Does he know I'm here?' Sylvie asked.

'I told him you were coming down, yes.'

'Then he can get in touch with me if he wants to, can't he?'

'I think he's too nervous.'

'Nervous?'

'He doesn't know what sort of reception he'd get.'

'Reception? I'm his daughter, not a werewolf.'

'So go and see him.'

She didn't answer for a moment. 'What's he like these days?'

'He drives a current Mercedes-Benz. He lives in a penthouse.

He collects butterflies. He holds a black belt in karate. He speaks fluent Swahili.' Sebastian smiled. 'Or perhaps he does none of those things. Find out for yourself.'

'Do you see him often?'

'Once a month or so. We usually meet for dinner. He's got a favourite Malaysian place in Prahran. Or we talk on the phone or by email.'

'So you're close?'

'We agree on some things, disagree on others. I know what's happening in his life, to a degree. He knows a bit about me.'

'Do you like him?'

'Sylvie, Dad is a human being. Not a cartoon villain or however Mum has painted him. He's likable sometimes, other times he drives me crazy. He's complicated. Welcome to the world of parents. Do you like Mum?'

The million-dollar question. Did she? She admired her, enjoyed her company much of the time, found her frustrating, stimulating. 'I love her. She's my mother.'

'You ignored the question. Skilfully, though, I'll give you that. You're off the hook for now.'

He called for the bill. On the way home to his apartment they called into a bar for a nightcap. He made her laugh with stories about badly behaved actors he'd worked with. They didn't speak about their father or mother again.

Sylvie walked out into the hallway of Sebastian's apartment now and looked at the framed photographs once more.

One photo to the side caught her eye. It was an old black

and white of Mill, pictured sweeping the front verandah of her Newtown flat with a straw broom, squinting into the lens, her hair falling out of its bun as usual. Sebastian had stuck a Post-it note to the bottom of it: *Great-Aunt Mill prepares for her companion Sylvie's arrival.* He had stuck another note underneath a photo of Vanessa and Cleo arriving at an opening night in a limousine: *Heckle and Jeckle alight from their pumpkin and greet the masses.*

She recognised lots of the photos. Sebastian was famous for raiding cupboards and photo albums on visits home and taking whatever he wanted. He said it was because he was the product of a broken home, that he was psychologically disturbed and in constant need of reassurance and familiar objects around him.

He amazed her, how matter-of-fact, even jokey, he was about it. She remembered the time of the divorce with only a tight feeling in her chest. She'd known of course that her parents weren't happy together. There'd been no way of not knowing. Creative people like her parents had found creative ways to abuse and insult one another.

There were several photos of the two of them, though none together. The ones of her father looked recent. She looked at them closely. She hadn't seen him in the flesh since she was eight years old.

Her idea of him had constantly changed since that time, influenced by whatever she was reading or watching. As a child, she'd thought of him as an Uncle Quentin-type distracted scientist character from the *Famous Five* books. The missing Mr March from *Little Women*. The absent father in *The Railway Children*.

The real Laurence Devereaux had an oval-shaped face, grey curly hair and enquiring eyes. Sebastian was very like him. Sylvie had often been told how like Sebastian she was.

Which meant she was like her father too.

4

By the end of the first week of her trial run, Sylvie had learned one new thing about herself.

She was no good at relaxing.

She'd walked into the city centre every day, via the Botanic Gardens, taking a different path each time to get to know her way around. She'd contacted five real estate agents to get an idea about current rents in nearby suburbs. She'd rung three temp agencies, emailed her CV and Sydney references to them all, done face-to-face interviews with two, a phone interview with the other one and was now on call for work with all three.

She'd asked herself a hundred questions and had a head full of possible answers. If I stayed here permanently, which suburb would I live in? What work would I do? Would I make any friends? Where would I eat out? Where would I stop for coffee after work? Where would I have long Sunday break-fasts? Where would I shop? Go dancing? See films? Underneath all of them was one big question: Would I be the same person I am in Sydney?

Sebastian rang to see how she was getting on. He was on location in an old country mansion halfway between Melbourne and Adelaide, working on a period drama. He was appalled when she told him what she'd been doing.

'What happened to the holiday? You're there to take some time out too, remember, not launch yourself on a full-scale reconnaissance mission.'

'It's a trial run. I'm trial running.'

'You're like an athlete on steroids. Slow down, would you? You have to have a gap in your life if you want something new to come in. Have you read a book? Watched a film? Listened to some calming music?'

'I haven't had time.'

He laughed. 'Then make time. And will you promise me something?'

'Depends.'

'Be home tomorrow between noon and one.'

'Why?'

'Just promise.'

She did as she was told. She got up early the next day, went to the shops down the road and bought all the ingredients for a leisurely holiday-type breakfast: fresh orange juice, warm croissants, ripe peaches and two newspapers. She read them from front to back. She took out the folder Sebastian had left for her, labelled *Possible Leisure Activities and Cultural Pursuits for Sylvie in my Absence*. There were theatre programs, cinema schedules, opening times for the nearby swimming pool, library, gym and video store, all with Post-it notes and comments attached. She made a list of things she'd like to see.

Tucked underneath them all, she found an old-fashioned luggage label. 'Pin this to your clothes every time you go out', he'd written on another Post-it note. The label read: *My name is Sylvie. I live on Marne Street, South Yarra. I am lost. Please look after me.* She grinned as she attached it to her red denim jacket, feeling like Paddington Bear.

By eleven o'clock she was fidgety. At work by this time, she would have made twenty phone calls, sent thirty emails, filled a dozen orders and probably booked her mother or sisters into either a restaurant, a beautician or their latest fad, Club Dance, a mid-morning exercise class in a nearby nightclub. Sylvie had read the brochure as she booked her sisters in for a six-week course. For a small fortune, they were being promised new levels of fat-burning and mood-lifting. When Sylvie wondered out loud if this was just a clever way of using the club during daylight hours, she'd been subjected to eye-rolling and accusations of being *so* pedestrian.

Maybe there was something to it. She was on her own, in Melbourne, it was light outside and she was sober, but too bad. She found a *Best of the 80s* CD in Sebastian's large collection.

From what she'd seen, all her neighbours left for work early, so she hoped for no complaints. She pushed back the furniture in the living room, turned the music up loud and danced to Dexy's Midnight Runners' 'Geno' and Spandau Ballet's 'Gold'. Midway through a Duran Duran song, the polished floorboards gave her an idea. She took off her sneakers and started sliding from room to room in her sock-covered feet. She changed CDs, finding Ravel's 'Bolero' and turning that up full blast as well. She did both Torvill and Dean's actions, making herself laugh. She and Sebastian had loved floor-skating as children, until Fidelma laid carpet in the hallway and main rooms. The dust coming up through the floorboards made her sneeze, she'd said.

Sylvie hadn't heard from her mother since leaving Sydney. She'd almost rung her four times. Each time she'd stopped. Fidelma was probably still at her coastal retreat. With Ray. Painting. Meeting her dealer. There was the shimmer of hurt that her mother hadn't rung to see how she was getting on, but it was a feeling she'd become used to over the years. It wasn't malice on Fidelma's part, as Sebastian had pointed out. It was absentmindedness. It still hurt.

As she slid to a halt near the answering machine in the hall, the light was flashing. Two messages. She hadn't heard the phone ring over the music. She pressed the button.

'Great-Aunt Mill calling, Sylvie. I've had a marvellous idea. Would you please start keeping a note of some handy house-hold hints for me? All tried and tested. I'm getting forgetful so I think the best thing is to tell you when I think of them. Carla next door says I should buy one of those Dictaphone gadgets but I thought, no, that's silly. I can tell you and you're young and you'll remember for me. Denture-cleaning tablets are ideal for bleaching white table linen. So simple, isn't it? Thank you, Sylvie. No need to call back.'

The second message was from her sister Cleo. Her voice filled the hallway.

'Hi, Seb. Hi, Sylvie. Hope Melbourne's good. Sylvie, I can't find that dry-cleaning anywhere. We're back in Sydney for an opening night and I need my blue dress. Where did you put it?'

Sylvie hadn't put it anywhere. In the flurry of packing and getting ready to leave, she'd forgotten to get it. Oh, bloody hell. She could call a courier and ask them to collect it and drop it around to Cleo. They should be able to give it to her without the docket. She'd ring them first and —

She stopped. Or she could ring Cleo back and tell her she was sorry, she'd forgotten, but perhaps Cleo could collect her own dry-cleaning.

She dialled the number before she lost her nerve. She could almost hear her heart beating. Voicemail, please, voicemail. Her plea was answered. 'Cleo, it's Sylvie.' Her voice was croaky. She gave a little cough. 'Hi, all's great here. Sebastian's apartment is beautiful. The weather's good. Um, your dry-cleaning —' About to back down and say she'd organise it from there, she had a vision of Sebastian frowning at her, mouthing, 'Don't let them bully you. Stand up for yourself.'

159

She stood up straight. 'I'm sorry, but unfortunately I didn't get time to collect it. The docket's in the in-tray on the desk in the studio. Hope your holiday's going well. See you.'

She had to stop herself phoning back and apologising again. She went out for a walk around the block, away from the temptation. When she got back fifteen minutes later, there was another message.

She pressed the button. Cleo, again. 'Hi, Sylvie. Thanks for letting me know about the dry-cleaning. What a complete bloody pain in the backside. We're only in town for a few hours and I haven't got time to visit the dry-cleaners. I thought I could trust you to do that before you left.' A sigh. 'All right, look, don't worry about it, I'll do it myself. See you.'

Any mood-lifting the dancing had done was wiped out.

At exactly noon, the doorbell sounded. A tall, thin, red-haired woman about her own age was at the front door, dressed in a strappy top, skinny jeans and heels. Sylvie barely had time to say hello before the other woman started talking.

'Sylvie? Of course you're Sylvie, who else? I'm Leila, Seb's neighbour across the courtyard.' She glanced down and her lips twitched. 'I like the name tag. Has it come in handy?'

Sebastian's label was still pinned to Sylvie's jacket. She hurriedly unpinned it, realising she'd also been for a walk around the block wearing it. 'It's a joke, I promise. Seb's idea of a joke, at least.'

'What's got into him lately? I spent a day last week with a Post-it note saying "I'm a monkey, give me a banana" on my back. He thought it was hilarious.'

'I'm so sorry. We thought the electric shock treatment was working.'

Leila smiled again, a dimple appearing in her cheek. 'Time to up the voltage, I think.' She took an envelope out of her bag. 'He asked me to drop this in to you today.'

Sylvie glanced at it, front and back. No clues there. 'Thanks very much.'

'Seb says you're down for a few weeks or maybe longer, is that right? Fancy a drink or something some night?'

'I'd love that, thanks.' Leila reminded Sylvie of someone. Pippi Longstocking, she realised, one of her favourite childhood book characters. She warmed to her even more. 'Would you like a coffee or something now?'

'Normally, yes please. I live on coffee. But I'm running late for an audition.' She pulled a face. 'I'm up for a part in one of the soaps today, hence this charming outfit. Another time maybe?'

'That'd be great, drop in any time. And good luck with the audition.'

'I need it, believe me. See you!' With a cheery wave, she was down the stairs and away.

Leila's visit cancelled out the effect of Cleo's phone message. Envelope in hand, Sylvie turned on the music again and went for a final slide around the apartment. As Talk Talk's

'It's My Life' came to an end, she arrived in the kitchen, took out a knife and carefully slit open the envelope.

Inside was a sheet of fax paper. On it, four lines in Sebastian's handwriting. Not last-minute instructions about the house-sitting. Nor tips about good restaurants or cafés or job websites or house agencies.

Sylvie smiled. It was something even better.

By mid-afternoon, the kitchen table was littered with scraps of paper covered in scribbles. There was a pile of books on the floor. Sylvie was on the phone.

'I can't figure it out, Seb. You have to give me a clue.'

It had taken her an hour to get hold of him. It was a bad line. 'Sorry, no can do, Miss Devereaux,' he said, his voice breaking in and out. 'It's a treasure hunt, not a treasure-handed-to-you-on-a-plate.'

'But I can't decipher the riddle. And I've been through every book on your bookshelf.' She'd opened every single one and there were no slips of paper to be found.

'That's cheating going straight to the books. You're supposed to look when you've deciphered the title, not flick through willy-nilly.'

'I was getting desperate. We can change the rules, can't we?'

'The rules are set in stone and shall be forever more. Apart from the fact I had to fax this starter clue down to Leila, but these were extraordinary circumstances. Anyway, who said anything about my bookshelf?'

'Where else should I look for a book? In the fridge?'

'Oh, you wit. There are other places for books, you know.'

'Libraries, you mean? You want me to go to the library?'

He lapsed into a Scottish accent. 'Och, pet, there are other places than libraries.'

Scottish. When had she heard a Scottish accent recently? Donald in the bookshop. 'The bookshop? Do you mean your friend's bookshop?'

'Is that the time? Got to go, Sylvie.' He hung up.

She pulled on her sneakers, picked up her bag and jacket and set off. The area already seemed familiar. Quiet roads lined with elegant stone houses beside modern apartments, all leading to the long shopping street. The sky was blue, but there was an autumn crispness to the air and a few brown leaves crunching underfoot.

As she walked, she thought back to the first of Sebastian's treasure hunts, a present for her eighth birthday. She remembered it so clearly, the one lovely thing in a time of turmoil. For the months beforehand, the mood in the family house had been an unhappy one. Her parents always seemed to be fighting. Odd things started happening. Sylvie's favourite painting of a small boat, an inheritance from Fidelma's grandmother, disappeared off the living room wall. So did the gold lamp in the hallway. Her father started staying out all night, coming home as Sylvie was on her way to school. He left one night with a suitcase. That time he didn't come back for a week. Her mother was either crying or angry all the time. She stayed in bed or sat on the back verandah. She rarely went into the studio. If she did, her paintings were angry splashes of colour, dark lines, fierce shapes.

Sylvie's birthday arrived. There was the present of a jigsaw puzzle, unwrapped, but no party and no cake. Her mother told her she was sorry, but she couldn't manage it. Vanessa and Cleo were otherwise occupied. Already a tight duo, they spent most of their time in their shared bedroom talking make-up and fashion, or out with their friends. There was no point asking them to help her make a birthday cake. Sebastian returned home late that night from an interstate theatre camp. He noticed there were no party leftovers. She heard him go in to their mother, heard raised voices. 'She's only a little kid. Couldn't you have done *something* special for her?' She didn't hear her mother's reply.

The next day Sylvie woke to find an envelope with her name on it at the end of her bed. A sheet of paper was inside. She opened it. It was Sebastian's writing.

A chair that grows wings?
Lands of pixies and elves?
If you want the next clue,
Better look on the shelves!

It took her nearly an hour to figure it out. Sebastian wouldn't help. 'It's a treasure hunt, Sylvie. You have to work it out.' She eventually realised what it meant. A chair with wings. The wishing chair. It was the name of one of her favourite Enid Blyton books. She found it on her bookshelf. She looked at the front cover, on the back. No clues there. She flicked through the pages. There, tucked in the middle, was another slip of paper. On it, two sentences of jumbled words:

Og ot het ozo. Kool ta eth gritse.

It took her an hour to figure them out, too. 'Go to the zoo? Look at the tigers?' she asked Sebastian. 'Is that what it says?'

'If that's what it says, then we'd better do it. Come on.'

They caught the ferry across the harbour and then a bus to the top of the hill. At the zoo, in front of the tigers' enclosure, he gave her another slip of paper. It told her to go to the café. They had chips and an ice-cream, as directed. Another slip of paper. To the harbour for another ferry ride, to Manly this time. Another slip of paper. To a bookshop. There behind the counter was a parcel with her name on it. Five Enid Blyton books. It was the best birthday of her life.

Until they got home that night and heard the news. Their parents were getting divorced.

Things grew worse. She heard her mother talking to her friends in her studio, using words she didn't understand.

Division of assets. Maintenance payments. Custody battles. As a child, she'd thought they were saying custardy. Fighting over custard? Why would they do that? Sebastian explained it to her. The family was going to be divided up.

The idea terrified her. 'I want to be with you, Sebbie. Wherever you are.'

'Sylvie, it won't be up to me.'

'Please, Seb. Please let me go with you.'

She was taken into an office, a room with a high ceiling and five red chairs. A woman behind a desk asked her in a kind voice where she would like to live. She didn't have to think twice. 'I want to be with my brother.'

'And if your brother was living with your father?'

'I want to be with my brother.'

In the end it didn't matter what she said. The judge decided. Sebastian was going to live with his father in Melbourne. Laurence Devereaux had been appointed to a position in the English department at Melbourne University. Fidelma was given custody of her three daughters, Vanessa, Cleo and Sylvie Devereaux. Case closed.

The day at the courtroom was the last time she'd seen her father. He'd come over to her and leaned down as if he was about to speak. Sylvie's mother took the top of her arm in a tight hold and pulled her away. There had been a bruise there the next day.

Sylvie reached Donald's bookshop, nestled between a French bakery and a wine shop. The front windows featured beautifully displayed books and posters. An old-fashioned bell sounded as she pushed open the glass door.

Without Sebastian sweeping her along beside him, she had more time to look around the shop. Pale wood shelves, a skylight, the walls painted calm colours, each section clearly marked: fiction, non-fiction, Australian, new releases, poetry, classics. Two tables at the front of the shop featured staff picks, recently reviewed titles and special promotion titles. To the side was a children's section divided not into fiction or non-fiction but into subjects: cats, dogs, trains, trucks. Classical music played softly. The whole shop smelt of coffee. Towards the back was a small café with three tables, armchairs and a compact coffee-making machine, the shelf above it lined with colourful cups and large glass jars filled with biscuits. There were half a dozen customers browsing the shelves and book tables.

The only assistant was up a ladder, putting up a poster. As she waited by the counter, he descended. She saw black runners. Long legs in faded jeans. A blue T-shirt. Lightly tanned arms. A head of dark-brown curls. It wasn't Donald.

The man turned as he reached the floor. He had a boyish sprinkling of freckles on his face. Dark eyes. A grown-up Huckleberry Finn, Sylvie thought. First Pippi Longstocking, now this man. She felt like she'd stumbled into Book Land at the top of the Faraway Tree.

He smiled at her. 'Hi. Sorry to keep you waiting. Can I help you?'

'Hello. Yes please. I was wondering if Dona—'

He interrupted. 'You're Sylvie, aren't you? Sebastian's sister?' At her nod he gave a big smile. 'He said you'd be calling in. You're exactly as he said you'd be.'

She wondered what Sebastian had said. Lost-looking? Anxious? She put on a bright expression, just in case. 'Which means you must be Max.'

He bowed. 'At your service. How did you know? Let me guess, he described me as a devastatingly good-looking man of the world?'

She smiled. 'Nearly. He said you were a very good friend of his.'

'And I am, for my sins.' He put out a hand. 'It's great to meet you. Are you looking for a book or a coffee? Both, maybe?'

'Actually, something a bit more complicated than that.'

'Excellent.' He leaned against the counter and folded his arms. 'I'm in the mood for something a bit more complicated today. Ask away.'

She reached into her bag for the envelope. 'When we were young, Sebastian and I used to —'

'You're on to the treasure hunt already?'

'You know about it?'

'I couldn't possibly say. But you don't waste any time, I'll give you that.'

She took out the piece of paper. 'He's left me the starter clue but I —'

Max put his hands over his ears and shut his eyes. 'Sorry, I can't help you.'

'You can't?'

He shook his head, eyes still shut. 'Seb said no matter how much you begged, you had to figure it out for yourself.'

'But can you tell me if I'm in the right place? Will I find the book here?'

He opened one eye. 'We've got twenty thousand books here so the odds are good. Any questions about them, feel free to ask. Though perhaps not twenty thousand questions this afternoon. We close at seven.'

'Can you help me at all?'

'I'm a highly trained bookshop assistant, with a mind like a computer; of course I can help you. But only with book-specific questions.'

She liked the spark of mischief in his eyes. If he was Sebastian's new partner, then she approved completely. 'Did you have a hand in this?'

Another grin. 'Let me just say that when Sebastian burns the midnight oil or gets a notion about doing something, he doesn't like doing it on his own. And that's the last bit of information you're getting. How about a coffee before you get started?'

'Could you make it a strong one?'

Ten minutes later, settled at a table at the back of the shop, a double espresso in front of her, she went over Sebastian's clue again. She'd read it so many times she knew it off by heart.

In search of a new and glittering vocation?
Then, dear Sylvie, travel old-fashioned kilometres
Across an ancient story-filled river.

His message was clear. He was telling her she needed to leave Sydney – the 'fashion' in 'old-fashioned' referred to Vanessa, the 'glittering' to Cleo's jewellery, she'd guessed – to find what she was supposed to be doing with her life. But what river had she crossed – or flown over at least – to get from Sydney to Melbourne? The Murray? Was she supposed to look in books about the Murray River?

Max was serving an elderly man. She waited a little back from the counter watching him. He had a lovely manner with the customer – friendly but respectful. He looked over and smiled at her as the man left.

'You've solved the puzzle already?'

'Inching closer every minute. I think I'm onto something. Would you have any books set on or about the Murray River?'

'Fiction or non-fiction? Or friction or non-friction, as my grandmother used to say.'

Sylvie smiled. 'Either. All. Any.'

He was very helpful. He checked on the computer, flicked through catalogues, searched the shelves with her. They found two fiction titles quickly: *The River Kings* by Max Fatchen and *All the Rivers Run* by Nancy Cato. There were also five works of non-fiction. She flicked through the pages of each of them. Nothing.

'It wouldn't have fallen out, would it?' she asked. 'It's usually only a little slip of paper.'

'I have no idea what you're talking about.'

'How long would it take me to check every book on every shelf here, do you think?'

'I've just done a part-time, manual stocktake so I can tell you – three weeks, two days and one long, heart-breaking final hour. Isn't that cheating, though? And have you got that long?'

'Would you mind me working through the night?'

'Of course not. You can sleep in the poetry section if you need to.'

'Is that a clue? It's in the poetry section?'

'No, I was trying to be funny. The poetry section being the quietest place.' He gave a rueful smile. 'Not that funny, obviously. I need new material.'

'No, it was. It was funny. I was laughing on the inside.'

He assumed a sad expression. 'If you're looking for me, I'll be in the comedy self-help section.'

She returned to the café, still smiling. She read the clue again. It was definitely more complicated than the ones they'd done as children. But the principle was the same, surely. Break it down, Sebastian used to say. Line by line. Make lists of all the possibilities.

She found a book on geography, listing dozens of terms for measuring distances. Furlongs. Roods. Perch. Miles. Yards. She wrote them down. Australian rivers? Darling. Torrens.

Swan. Fitzroy. Franklin. Yarra. Margaret. *Margaret*. The author's first name? She underlined it.

She consulted dictionaries, thesauruses, atlases and guide-books. When he wasn't serving customers and unpacking boxes, Max kept her supplied with coffee. He refused any money. 'It's all on Sebastian's tab. Whatever you want. He insisted.'

She listed words for glittering and vocation. Shining. Bright. Brilliant. Clear. Glossy. Luminous. Silver. Radiant. Job. Occu-pation. Career. Vocation. Duty. Position. Trade. Work.

Nothing. Just a swirl of words in her brain. She decided to distract herself with a quick walk and some fresh air and hope her subconscious would take over. It often worked when she was doing cryptic crosswords.

Max was at the counter, serving a customer. She mouthed that she'd be back in a moment and got a nod and smile in reply.

She was barely six shops away, just beyond the Italian restau-rant, when it came to her. *Glittering vocation. Old-fashioned kilometres. Ancient river*. She ran back to the bookshop and threw open the door.

'*My Brilliant Career* by Miles Franklin,' she shouted.

The man at the counter looked up in surprise. Not Max, but Donald. 'Sylvie, how nice to see you again.'

5

'So if I decided on the spur of the moment to hold a conference for five hundred people in four different languages and needed a fleet of secretaries, I could call you and you'd organise and manage the whole thing for me? Take shorthand? Work the computers? Organise everything?'

'Blindfolded,' Sylvie said, laughing. 'Arms tied behind my back.'

'That might make typing tricky, but never mind. You're not a secretary, you're Supertemp. Mental note, Max. If in need of a multilingual conference, call Sylvie immediately.'

They'd been in the bar together for the past hour. Five doors down from the bookshop, it was small and Spanish-themed, with tapas on offer, flamenco music playing quietly in the background, and brightly coloured walls and dim lamps creating an intimate atmosphere. She noticed his empty glass. 'It's your turn to answer questions. As soon as I get you another glass of wine.'

'My life is an open book. Very dull.' He stood up. 'And I got off work early because of you, so the drinks are on me. Same again?'

She nodded. It had been Donald's idea for the two of them to go for a drink. He'd been very amused after she'd launched herself through the door of his shop, startling not only him but also his customers. Max had emerged laughing from behind the non-fiction shelves.

Donald waved away her apologies. 'It's nice to see someone so enthusiastic about their reading matter. Let me see, if my highly tuned intuition as a bookseller is right, you're quite interested in taking a look at *My Brilliant Career* by Miles Franklin? Now, where would that be, I wonder? Max, have you seen it?'

'I think we sold the last copy,' Max said. 'Just after Sylvie went for her walk.'

'Never mind. We could put an order in. An Australian classic like that, let me think, I could have it in within the week?'

'You're tormenting me now,' Sylvie said. 'I'm calling Consumer Affairs.'

'Sebastian was right about her, wasn't he, Donald?' Max said. 'How was it he described her to us? "A bright-eyed cutie?"'

'That was it. But he certainly didn't mention her habit of shouting book titles at the top of her voice. They obviously have different shopping habits in Sydney. Max, loyal assistant, could you please show this bright-eyed young lady to our classics section?'

The Fs were on the second row from the top. Max reached up easily and took down the only copy. 'Shall I wrap that for you, madam? Or will you be ripping straight into the pages here and now?'

'Right here and now, thank you.'

She found the slip of paper in seconds. It was in the centre pages, folded in three. Sebastian had kept up the tradition of their childhood treasure hunts. There was a whole page of writing, all in jumbled letters. She looked up. Max was smiling at her.

'Did you know it was here the whole time?' she asked.

He nodded. 'I put it there. Sebastian couldn't reach.'

'So I could have bribed you when I came in this morning?'

'It would have been quicker. But look at all the practice you gave me making coffee. And now I'm an expert on the Murray River. That kind of knowledge can't be bought.'

He returned from the bar now with two glasses of wine. 'Here you are,' he said. 'A fine fruity shiraz from the Yarra Valley. Or perhaps it's a spicy cabernet from the Clare Valley. Or a cheeky full-bodied merlot from the Hunter Valley. I can't remember. It's a glass of red wine, anyway.'

'My favourite kind. Thanks, Max.'

He settled into his seat opposite her again.

'So, the trip to Melbourne is —' he said.

'So do you like working in the —' she asked.

They both laughed. 'You first,' Max said.

'I was going to ask if you liked working in the bookshop. And if you're originally from Melbourne.'

'Excellent questions, thank you. If you had asked them, I would have said yes to both before skilfully turning the conversation on its head and asking you what it was like to grow up in the middle of an artistic family like yours.' He paused. 'And then I would realise from the expression on your face that you've been asked that question far too many times and that is, of course, one of the reasons you left Sydney, so I would hurriedly backtrack and ask you an innocuous question about the weather.'

'Sorry. It was that obvious?'

He nodded. 'You've got one of those faces that gives a lot away. You'd make a good actress.'

'If I could act, yes.'

'You never tried?'

She shook her head. 'I can't paint, make jewellery or design clothes either, in case you were going to ask.'

'I wasn't, but that's good to know. I can't either, as it happens.'

She rubbed at her cheek, embarrassed. 'Sorry, Max. That wasn't fair.'

'Dr Max Reynolds, Family Therapist, is now in session. Would you like an appointment?'

She wanted to talk to him about it, she realised. 'Have you got a few hours?'

'Days, if needed. And they've got loads of wine behind the bar. I checked.'

'I don't know how much Sebastian told you —'

'Nothing too incriminating, I promise. He said he thought you were drowning in a sea of family, so he threw you a lifeline.'

'That's it in a nutshell. Embarrassing, isn't it? Nearly thirty and still being looked after by my big brother.'

'Not so big. What is he, five foot seven? A titch. A titch brother. And don't be embarrassed about it. We need our families to drive us crazy. Otherwise no one would ever go anywhere and what would get done in the world?'

'You think that?'

'I know it.'

'It's the same for you?'

He nodded. 'I'm the oldest of three boys. Mum and Dad are both doctors, with their own practice. There were expectations, obligations really, that I would become a doctor too.' He'd enrolled for med school before he knew it, he told her. Graduated, worked in the practice, knowing the whole time something was wrong. 'Then about four years ago I joined an amateur theatre group and that's when I realised what I wanted. Stage sets and scripts, not stethoscopes or charts. The production side, not the acting. The next week I enrolled to do stage management at the college of the arts. I've worked in theatre ever since. It's more precarious than medicine, but I love it.'

'So the bookshop is a part-time job?'

He nodded. 'Three days a week. It keeps me going between plays. That's how I met Sebastian. We worked on a production together last year. In fact, he got me the job in the bookshop. He's very good at looking after people.'

'And how did changing direction go down with your family? Your parents?'

'They loved it. Thought it was a fantastic idea.' He gave a quick smile. 'They were furious. I was ignored for a few months. Shouted at for another month. Four generations of the family in medicine. Who did I think I was, breaking with tradition? I needn't think they'd support me, etcetera etcetera.'

'Your brothers weren't interested either?'

'Not four years ago. It's changed now. My youngest brother's applied to do medicine, so my parents are mollified for the moment.' He gave a shrug. 'There it is. I can't condemn them for it. They're traditional. Old-fashioned. They also care too much what other people think about them. Social standing, that kind of thing.'

She'd had too much wine to be diplomatic. 'But they're okay about you and Sebastian?'

'Sorry?'

'About the two of you?'

'The two of us?'

'Being a couple.'

'Sebastian and I being a couple?' At her nod, he threw back

his head and laughed. 'You thought Sebastian and I were together?'

'Aren't you?'

'Where did you get that idea?'

'He said that you were a very good friend of his and he had a kind of glint in his eye.'

'A glint?' He grinned. 'Sylvie, I'm sorry. Much as I'd love to be your brother-in-law, Sebastian and I bat for different teams. And as far as I can tell, Sebastian and Donald are very happy together without me interfering.'

'Donald?'

'Donald and Sebastian are together. You didn't know?'

'He said he was seeing someone. I got it into my head that it was you . . .'

Max laughed again. 'That's it. Tomorrow I start growing a beard. Taking body-building classes. Injecting testosterone.'

'I didn't . . . I hope you don't . . . You didn't seem . . .' She stopped trying. 'Sorry.'

'It's fine. It means I'm in touch with my sensitive side. That's a good thing, surely.'

'A very good thing.'

'No harm done, then. Come on, let's get out of here.'

'Where are we going?'

'To a lap-dancing club. I've got a few things to prove.' He grinned at her expression. 'No, not a lap-dancing club. I'm taking you to dinner. I've got a lot of ground to make up.'

*

As they walked two blocks away to a small Greek restaurant, the mood changed between them. Over dinner, there was more conversation, occasional quick touches on each other's sleeves or hands. Either Max felt he had something to prove, or they had naturally tipped from conversation into a kind of flirting. Sylvie wasn't sure. All she knew was it had changed from being a night out with her brother's partner to feeling something more like a date. It was a very good feeling.

He walked her home afterwards. The restaurant was only ten minutes from Sebastian's apartment. The houses were mostly dark, a few cars driving down the side streets, a chill in the air. They stopped at the front of the apartment building. There were lights on behind curtains, the faint sound of a cello drifting down through an open window.

Max looked up at Sebastian's apartment and sighed. 'Ah, my love nest. My heart pounds to think of the nights I've spent there.'

'I'm sorry, I promise you. Which of us will ring Seb first and tell him, do you think?'

'I'll leave that to you. Give him my love, won't you?' He laughed. 'I mean it. I do love Sebastian.'

'I'm sure he loves you too.'

'I really enjoyed tonight, Sylvie. Drop in to the shop any time. Or give me a ring at home if you feel like a coffee.' He scribbled a number on the back of a receipt. 'I work odd hours so I'll be free when you least expect it.'

'And me too. I mean, ring here if you want to as well.

Thanks, Max. For the wine and dinner and everything.'

'You're very welcome.' He touched the side of her face, a quick, sweet gesture. 'It's nice to have you here.'

'It's nice to be here.' A moment where they smiled at each other. A moment when she wanted to say, What about a drink tomorrow night? Or dinner at the end of the week? She left it too long. 'Goodnight.'

She turned as she reached the top of her stairs. He was still there. He raised a hand in a wave.

She rang Sebastian as soon as she got inside. He laughed at the case of mistaken identity. He was very glad she'd found the clue. He was also glad at the news of her drink and dinner with Max.

'Are you matchmaking, Seb?'

'Not actively,' he said. 'Just letting chemistry do its work. I like Max, I like you, therefore I assumed if I put Max with you, you would like each other. And being the magician I am, it happened. Prince Charming rides into your life.'

'But I'm not looking for Prince Charming.'

'Of course you're not. You've got far more serious problems than your love life.'

'Thanks very much.'

'I just thought it might be nice for you to meet someone who isn't a stinking deceitful social-climbing two-timing bastard like David. That's how you summed him up, wasn't it?'

'I think you left out two-faced.'

She still felt stupid thinking about David. It had taken her five months with him before she realised it was her Devereaux surname he was interested in, not her. She'd met him at one of her mother's exhibition openings. A lawyer studying art history in his spare time, he'd been full of opinions and talk of reviving the artistic salon tradition. He'd swept Sylvie off her feet. Her mother and sisters had been hugely flattered by his attention too. They'd come to the parties he'd thrown, cheerfully posed for the society photographers who often seemed to turn up. It took Sylvie far too long to realise what was going on. The clincher was when he began introducing her not as 'my girlfriend Sylvie', but as 'my dear friend Sylvie, one of the Devereaux family of artists'.

She'd brought it up on the way back to his apartment in Double Bay one night. 'I don't know why you keep saying that, David. I'm not an artist.'

'I can hardly introduce you as just a secretary, can I?'

She finished it with him that night. He pursued her with flowers and apologies until she gave him a second chance. He threw another party to celebrate. He invited her family again and spent most of the night talking to Fidelma. It ended when Sylvie saw a photo of him in the Sunday gossip pages, photographed beside the daughter of a well-known Sydney actor. He'd told Sylvie he was working back late that night. That time he accepted it was over. The next day he sent flowers to Fidelma, Vanessa and Cleo, saying it had been a pleasure to meet each of them. He sent them to the office. Sylvie was the only one there. She'd had to sign for them.

'And you liked Donald?' Sebastian said now.

She could hear the vulnerable tone in his voice. 'I liked him very much.'

'Good.' He was smiling now. She could hear that too. 'That's very good. Now get to bed. You've a lot of un-puzzling to do in the morning.'

It wasn't until after she'd cleaned her teeth and was about to get into bed that she checked the answering machine. It was flashing. One message. Max, she thought. Leaving a message already. She pressed the button.

'Sylvie, Mill here. Two quick thoughts. White vinegar makes a marvellous fabric softener. Just add a quick splash to the final rinse. And cider vinegar added to chooks' drinking water stops them getting worms. All for now. Goodnight. No need to call back.'

6

It took Sylvie one pot of coffee, two chocolate croissants and one-and-a-half hours the next morning to un-jumble the dares. By Sebastian's standards, they were mild. No leaping off tall buildings. No eating of worms or spiders or caterpillars.

He'd set her three dares. She could spread them out over the next week or get the whole lot over and done with in a day. It was up to her. He wanted full reports, preferably typed or in Powerpoint form, but he would also settle for quick calls or messages left on his mobile phone. He would prefer it if she did them in the order listed but he gave her permission to be flexible.

The list was titled Sylvie's Three-Step Search for Certainty.

One: Ask someone out on a date.

Two: Host a dinner party. Dishes must contain the following ingredients: coriander, fish sauce, sesame oil, chilli, rice wine, galangal, lemongrass and Kaffir lime leaves.

Three: To be divulged when dares one and two are successfully completed.

The phone rang before she had a chance to start thinking about them. She snatched it up before it went to the answering machine. It was Mill.

'Oh, what a shame to get you, Sylvie,' she said immediately. 'I've really started to prefer answering machines. So much more efficient. No need to ask how are you, what have you been doing, how's the weather, etcetera, don't you find? You can get straight to the point.'

'I can hang up if you like.'

Mill gave a roar of laughter. 'That would teach me. I must say I do like that cheeky little spirit of yours. I was just talking about you, in fact. Telling George here that you're coming to live with me when you get back from Melbourne.'

'George?'

'My new gardener. Marvellous man. Strong and hardy, like a plant himself. He said you sounded nice too. He's surprisingly knowledgeable about all sorts of things, not only plants. Quite the antiques expert. Says I'm sitting on some valuable objects here. I'm not surprised. Vincent had a wonderful eye.'

An alarm bell rang. 'Mill, who is this George?'

'George. Of George's Gorgeous Gardens. He's perfectly legitimate. Large ad in the Yellow Pages. A website even, he tells me. Not that I'm too sure what that is.'

Sylvie decided she'd check it out as soon as possible. But in the meantime . . . 'Mill, please don't tell people I'm coming to live with you.'

'You want to keep it a secret? No problem at all. I was saying to George that the blue room is definitely the best one for you, but he said we might get bats in the Moreton Bay out the front, or even the occasional funnel web. You wouldn't mind them, would you? You don't look the squeamish, timid type to me.'

'Mill, I don't know how to make this any clearer, but I'm not planning on coming back to Sydney for a while. Possibly ever. I'm looking for work here.'

'I understand completely. Just let me know when you're due back and I'll get someone to meet you at the airport. Now, I'd better give you today's tip. When you're frying eggs, sprinkle a little bit of flour in the hot oil. It stops any spatters. Bye for now, Sylvie.'

That hadn't gone right, Sylvie thought, looking down at the phone. The call had warmed her up, though. Before there was time to think, she took out the piece of paper with Max's number on it and dialled.

It rang six times before a man answered. Was it him? She didn't know his voice well enough. 'Max?'

'Sylvie, I was just thinking about you.'

'You were?'

'I was going to ring and ask if you wanted to meet me for a drink at the end of the week.'

Drat, he'd got in first. She needed to ask him out on a date. Did it count that she was the one who had rung him?

'Sylvie, are you there? I've asked you for a drink, not a round-the-world cruise. Just say yes.'

The laughter in his voice gave her nerve. 'Max, I'm sorry, but can you hang up and then answer it again when I ring?'

'I could, if you truly think that makes any sense.'

'I'll explain why later.'

'I'll look forward to that.' He hung up.

She dialled the number again. 'Max?'

'Sylvie, hello. Who'd have thought? How are you today?' He sounded like a detective trying to talk a mad person off a window ledge.

'Would you like to meet me for a drink on Friday night?'

'What a lovely idea. I wish I'd thought of it myself.'

She crossed the dare off the list. 'Thank you very much. Seven o'clock? The Spanish bar? Great, see you then.'

She hung up. She felt great. Really great. And not only because she'd already done one of her dares.

There was a knock at the front door just after three o'clock. It was Leila. She didn't waste time with pleasantries. 'That coffee you mentioned the other day. I don't suppose it's still up for grabs?'

'Of course, come in. How did it go?'

'The soap audition? It was disastrous.'

'What happened?'

'Self-sabotage.' Leila gave a big sigh as she followed Sylvie into the kitchen. 'Something got into me about two minutes after I arrived and I couldn't stop giggling. Which would have been fine if it had been a girly part, but I was going for the part of a newly widowed young mother. I read the lines as if it was the most hilarious thing that had ever happened to me.'

'Oh, Leila.'

' "Oh, Leila" is right. And do you know what made it worse? I heard them talking about it afterwards. They said it was the worst audition they'd ever seen. The producer said that one is definitely going on the bloopers tape. I don't blame them. You should have seen me. *"He's dead? My husband's dead? But how will I go on without him?"* And me laughing as if I've inhaled a hot-air balloon full of laughing gas.'

'It must have been nerves.'

'Not nerves. The gods telling me to find a new career. Sylvie, do you have any cigarettes?'

'Sorry, no. I don't smoke.'

'Neither do I. I want to start, though. Forget the coffee. Do you have to do anything today? Will you come and get drunk with me? You didn't have anything else planned, did you?'

Sylvie thought of Sebastian's list. 'Actually, yes. A dinner party. For next Saturday night. Would you like to come?'

'Sure. If you come and get drunk with me now.'

'It's a deal.'

Six hours later, it took Sylvie five tries to get her key in the lock. It was nearly midnight. Her head was spinning from too much vodka, too much loud music and eight unaccustomed cigarettes. She squinted as she looked at the answering machine. No messages from Mill tonight. Oh, God. That reminded her. She'd meant to check the George's Gorgeous Gardens website. Some great-niece she was. Mill could be cut up in tiny pieces and buried under the flagstones of her newly gorgeous garden by now.

As she waited for Sebastian's computer to boot up, Sylvie went to the kitchen and made herself drink three large glasses of water. She caught sight of her reflection in the dark of the kitchen window. A panda looked back at her. She always ended up with mascara smudges under her eyes when she laughed. She'd spent most of the afternoon laughing.

'What Midas is to gold, I am to chaos,' Leila had announced as they walked to a bar she knew in Prahran. 'Everything I touch turns to ruin. I'm the original Calamity Jane. It's not funny, Sylvie. Stop smiling. I can't help it. I've been like it since I was a child.'

As they played pool, Leila entertained her with a litany of her disasters. Her first cubbyhouse, built by her farmer father in secret for her tenth birthday, swept away in a flash flood the day after her party. Her first day at high school ruined when she spent the day with her school uniform tucked into her knickers. Her step into independence, moving to Melbourne from a country town north of Ballarat as a 28-year-old, hitting a major road hump when the removal van carrying all her belongings caught fire en route. Her attempt to stave off loneliness in her first few months by volunteering to visit old people in their homes coming to an end when her allocated old lady sacked her for not being interesting enough. Her attempt to get fit ending in failure when her clothes were stolen from the side of the Harold Holt pool while she was swimming laps one winter afternoon. She'd had to catch the tram home wearing only her bathers.

'That's why it's good to hang around me,' Leila had said. 'I attract everybody else's share of bad luck as well as my own. Do you think I could hire myself out? As a kind of reverse good-luck charm?'

Still smiling at the memory, Sylvie carried a fourth glass of water into Sebastian's office and settled herself at the computer. After one or two vodka-fuelled spelling mistakes, she found the website for George's Gorgeous Gardens. It was professional, with photographs, a detailed profile of George himself and a long list of his qualifications. There were more than a dozen testimonials from happy clients. Good. It looked like Mill, and her garden, were in safe hands. Safe green thumbs, even.

In bed soon after, trying to get to sleep and ignore her spin-ning head, Sylvie remembered something else Leila had said that day. Something that didn't make her smile.

They'd been in the third bar of the day, playing their fourth game of pool, drinking their third or possibly fourth vodka and tonic. Sylvie had told Leila about the treasure hunt Sebas-tian had left, the clues leading to the bookshop and the list of dares. Pressed for more details, she'd told her about the situ-ation with her mother and sisters in Sydney, and all that had happened the night of Vanessa's wedding.

'I wish I had a big brother who cared about me like that,' Leila said. 'My three little brothers are demons. Heavy metal music-lovers. Motorbike addicts. If there's ever an earthquake in Victoria, the epicentre will be our house.' She expertly pot-ted three balls, then looked across the green table.

'Where's your father, Sylvie? You haven't mentioned him.'

'Here. In Melbourne.'

'They're divorced?'

Sylvie nodded.

'What happened?'

'Irreconcilable differences. Is that the legal term for scream-ing at each other all the time? He left when I was eight. Sebastian went with him.'

'Have you seen your dad since you've been down here?'

'I haven't seen him since I was eight.'

Leila stopped lining up her shot. 'Twenty years?'

'Twenty-one.'

'Why not?'

'Mum didn't want me to when I was younger. It would upset her too much if I suggested it. And since then . . .' She shrugged.

'Aren't you curious? Even to have a look at him?'

What she felt wasn't curiosity. It was hurt, wrapped up in years of no phone calls or birthday cards. 'It's too late now. And I still wouldn't like to upset Mum.' It sounded feeble even to her own ears.

'But you're an adult female. Your role in life as a daughter is to upset your mother. Didn't you know that? I drive my mother bananas.'

'It's more complicated than that.'

'You must be curious, though?'

Sylvie wanted to drop this topic. 'Of course. But he's always known where I was as well. It takes two.'

'I disagree. It takes one. One of you to make the first move.' They played two shots each before Leila spoke again. 'Can I ask you a blunt question?'

In Sylvie's experience, the best answer to an enquiry like that was usually no. 'Go ahead.'

'Have you ever thought about taking charge of your own life?'

'Pardon?'

Leila chalked the end of her cue, looking seriously over at Sylvie. 'I'm sorry if this comes out wrong, but the way you've told it, you've spent the past few years doing whatever your mother and sisters told you to do. Now you're down here doing what Sebastian wants you to do. Not just coming to Melbourne and minding his house, but this whole treasure hunt thing.'

'It's only a bit of fun.'

'I know. And I told you, I'd love a big brother who did something like this for me. But you're nearly thirty. When are you going to start making your own decisions? About life. About seeing your father. You're obviously bright, you're great company. I can't see why you haven't broken out on your own before now.'

Sylvie couldn't tell whether Leila was insulting or complimenting her. 'I haven't been sure what I wanted to do yet.'

'No? Fair enough.' Leila lined up the ball, played her shot. It missed. 'It's probably easier to let other people boss you around, then. Your turn, Sylvie.'

Leila's words kept going around her head. Is that what she'd been doing? Taking the easy way out by letting people boss her around? She hoped not. Wasn't it that she liked helping people? Being busy? Feeling needed? Or had she let it become an excuse?

It was past three before she got to sleep.

She rang her mother first thing the next morning, before she made coffee or tried to find some headache tablets. If she kept waiting for her to call, it might never happen. If she wanted to talk to her mother, then it was up to her to ring.

Fidelma sounded genuinely delighted to hear from her. 'Sylvie, darling, how are things? I was leaving you alone. You have enough of me in Sydney. I thought you might like the peace. Ray and I are back from the retreat and I feel truly inspired. I've already got ideas for my next exhibition. I do believe the landscape there speaks right to my inner self. Ray was up before dawn each morning meditating, and he agrees that being close to nature is so important, not just for our creativity but for our souls. I'm thinking of introducing a new element to my work, possibly multimedia, incorporating . . .'

When she hung up ten minutes later, Sylvie realised her mother had never actually heard how things were going for her in Melbourne or how she was feeling. Either Sylvie was still numb from all the vodka the day before, or she didn't mind as much as usual.

As she went out for a walk a little later her eyes were drawn once again to her father's photograph in the hallway. She stopped and looked at it.

What would they talk about if she did ring him? His poetry? The truth was she'd never really understood it. It was experimental, jagged, angry writing. What else had Sebastian said about him? That he spoke Swahili? Lived in a penthouse? Drove a new car? Or maybe none of those things?

It would be easy to find out. All she had to do was ring Sebastian and ask for her father's contact number. Get his address. Turn up on his doorstep and say, 'Hello, Dad. I'm your daughter.'

But what would happen then, she wondered. Where did you start with someone you hadn't seen for twenty-one years?

Leila didn't bother knocking when she called by later that afternoon.

'Are you dying of a hangover?' she called out. 'It's your own fault if you are. You should have said no when I asked you to come out with me.'

'I'm telling myself the same thing,' Sylvie said, looking up from her nest of cushions in the bay window. An empty can of Coke and bag of chips was beside her. 'I think it would be dangerous to be your friend.'

'That's why I don't have any friends. That, and my bad habit of speaking my mind. I do remember that right, don't I? I did tell you to get a grip on your own life last night?'

'You did, yes.'

'And I've only just met you. And I don't know the whole story. And who am I to tell you, with my own life a mess. That's what you thought, didn't you?'

'You're a mind reader as well as an actress?'

'A failed actress. Please use the correct terminology. Sorry, Sylvie. I was out of line. I was right, of course, but it wasn't my job to tell you.'

Sylvie liked Leila too much to be mad at her. And there was also the little matter of Leila possibly hitting the nail on the head . . . 'You're forgiven, I promise. Can I get you back, though? I'm meeting a friend for a drink on Friday night. Do you want to come along too?'

'How can you have another friend already? You've only just arrived in Melbourne. That's not fair. I've been here nearly two years and I hardly know anyone.'

'He's a friend of Seb's.'

'That brother of yours knows too many people. I can't come, as it turns out. I'm having dinner with friends in Carlton.'

'So you do have friends?'

'Only ones who feel sorry for me. I met this couple when I was doing some house-sitting last summer. I managed to set their chimney on fire. I know. Don't ask. But thanks anyway.'

'You're welcome. And thanks for last night.'

'Thanks for the hangover, you mean.' Leila gave her a cheery wave and a smile as she headed out again. 'See, I really am a mind reader!'

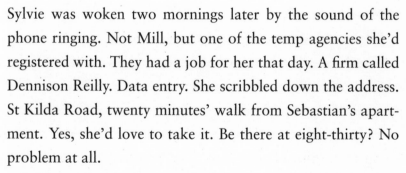

7

Sylvie was woken two mornings later by the sound of the phone ringing. Not Mill, but one of the temp agencies she'd registered with. They had a job for her that day. A firm called Dennison Reilly. Data entry. She scribbled down the address. St Kilda Road, twenty minutes' walk from Sebastian's apartment. Yes, she'd love to take it. Be there at eight-thirty? No problem at all.

It felt good to be in work clothes again, instead of the jeans and T-shirts she'd been living in the past week or so. She looked the image of efficiency: pencil skirt, crisp white shirt, pearl earrings and black pumps. She'd called into a hairdresser on Toorak Road the previous afternoon and had one of her best cuts in years. The corkscrew curls were now soft waves, close to her head. Gamine, the hairdresser told her. Whatever it was called, it had been easy to manage that morning.

She arrived at the large, glass-clad twenty-storey building on St Kilda Road at eight-twenty a.m. She had to sign in, then wait with fifteen other corporately clad people to be taken up seventeen floors to a warren of silent offices. A middle-aged woman came to the reception desk to collect Sylvie. Dark hair pulled back in a ponytail. A lot of makeup. A strong floral perfume. She didn't offer her name, or make any small chat.

Sylvie tried her best as she followed her along the corridor. 'You have a great view from up here.'

No answer.

'You're an insurance company, I believe?' She'd glanced at the brochures in the reception area.

The woman gave a nod.

Sylvie was shown to a small, windowless cubicle with a computer and five boxes of files. The supervisor didn't meet her eye once. She could have been showing a trained monkey around. She gestured to the computer, where a database was already up on screen. 'Update those files. Check the details against the files in that box.' She pointed again and then turned to leave.

'Please,' Sylvie said, with a bright smile.

There was eye contact then. 'What?'

It felt important to say something. 'I'm sorry, but I felt like you were telling me, not asking me.'

'I am telling you, not asking you. You're a temp.'

The woman left her then, shutting the door with something close to a slam behind her. After a moment wondering whether to curse or laugh, Sylvie made a start on the work. Compared to all the years with Executive Stress Relief, not to mention her time in the family studio, this felt like taking baby steps. Routine, repetitive and strangely restful. Her fingers flew across the keyboard as she rapidly input the information. She did a quick calculation. The temp agency might not be pleased commission-wise, but she could probably get through most of these files today.

Fifteen minutes later, Sylvie got a phone call. It was the agency.

'We've had a complaint, Sylvie. I'm surprised, because your references from Sydney were so excellent.'

'What kind of complaint?'

'You apparently have an attitude problem.'

'I do?'

'Our client said you were insolent and showed a lack of respect. She also reminded me, as I'll also tell you, that they are one of our best customers.'

There was no point going into it then. 'I'm sorry,' Sylvie said. 'I certainly didn't mean to be insolent.'

'Work through to lunchtime, would you? I'll send another temp in this afternoon.'

'You're taking me off the job?'

'She's asked us to. Demanded it.'

'That's fine,' Sylvie said calmly, outwardly professional, inwardly swearing. 'I'll keep working in the meantime.'

She got through almost a box of files by eleven-thirty,

before she realised she needed a coffee and a bathroom. The woman hadn't shown her where either was. Sylvie made her way down the corridor, peering into the offices. There was little chat, just heads down working. She found the woman at the end of the building, standing by the coffee machine.

'You're still here?' Not a 'Hello', not a 'Can I help you?'

'Just until lunchtime,' Sylvie said, trying to keep her voice and expression pleasant. 'I needed a coffee. Can I please help myself?'

The woman stepped to one side, still blocking the cups. 'Five minutes break, maximum.'

Sylvie made a coffee, pressing the buttons, watching the dart of instant coffee arrive in the cup. She thought of all the temp jobs she'd had, all the other temps she'd met, the different experiences of the job that she'd heard about. She remembered how well treated and respected she was by the Executive Stress Relief clients. As the other woman threw her empty cup into the bin and turned to leave, Sylvie seized her moment.

'Excuse me?'

The woman stopped.

'I hope you don't mind me saying, but I think you might be the one with the attitude problem here.'

'What?'

'Temps are human beings too. Not robots. I wasn't being insolent, I was asking to be treated with some respect and —'

'That's enough. Your five minutes' break is up. I hope you don't mind me saying.' The last was delivered in a sarcastic tone.

Sylvie was barely back in her cubicle when she got another phone call from the agency.

'She's asked for you to be removed now. We've got your replacement coming in urgently. We'll have to take you off our books, Sylvie. We can't have a loose cannon working for us.'

A loose cannon? Her? It felt like the biggest compliment she'd ever been paid. 'I understand completely,' she said.

Her bravado had faded by the time she walked home. Her shoes were pinching. Her shirt was sticking to her back. It was an unseasonally warm day. It didn't bode well for her future here in Melbourne if she was sacked from her first job.

The phone in the hallway was ringing as she let herself in. 'Sebastian's house.'

'Sylvie, I didn't expect to get you. I have another tip for you. Do you have paper and a pen?'

'Of course, Mill.' She reached into her bag for a notebook. 'Ready when you are.'

'You sound quite flat. Not yourself at all. What's wrong? Has something happened?'

'It has, yes.' Sylvie was surprised to hear herself say it. 'Just something silly.'

'It's the silly things that are often the most upsetting, in my experience. Tell me. I've been on my own in the house all day. I could do with a story.'

Sylvie told Mill everything that had happened in the insurance office. 'I keep wishing I'd said something else to her. Told the agency what she was like. I shouldn't have let her get away with it.'

'No, you shouldn't have,' Mill said. 'You should have set fire to all her files before you left.'

Sylvie laughed. 'Exactly. And then wiped out the computer program.'

'Yes. Then dialled the speaking clock in China on the office phone. Put a prawn inside her curtain rod. Let down her tyres. Offered her some laxative chocolates. Sprinkled itching powder in her hair.'

'They're not more of your handy household hints, are they?'

Mill laughed enthusiastically. 'No, but wouldn't it be fun to try them one day? I'm glad you're out of there, Sylvie. That woman sounds like a horrible stinking old bitch.'

'Mill!'

'Well, she does. I can't abide bullying behaviour. People trying to put others in their place. It's a sign of insecurity, you know. Something similar happened to me when I was your age. This particular gentleman used to turn up his nose at me when I would attend recitals with Vincent. "I don't know what he's doing out socially with his housekeeper," he said to me once. Looked down his nose. It's an apt expression, that one. So I lifted my chin one night and said, "I'm sensational in bed, as it happens." That shut him up. Though of course it went around like wildfire that I wasn't a housekeeper but some kind of a prostitute. Vincent thought it was hilarious. Would tell people he'd bought me on hire purchase.' She went off into peals of laughter.

'Mill, have you been drinking?'

'At this time of day, of course not. Cocktail hour is six p.m. Why do you young people assume we never had sex in our day? Surry Hills was as much a hotbed back then as it is now. Vincent was quite adventurous too, you know. He loved it when I —'

'Mill, please.'

'Oh, how marvellous. George has pulled up outside. He said he'd try and drop by today, even for a few minutes. He's doing wonders. Quite transforming the garden. Once you and I get started on the inside it'll be a whole new place. Did I give you today's tip, by the way?'

'No, not yet.'

'Cold cream. It's all a woman needs for her skin. That and a hat to keep the sun off. Speak to you soon, Sylvie.'

'Thanks, Mill, but —' It was too late. She'd already hung up.

Sylvie made a cup of tea, thought about it for a little while, and then rang the woman at the temp agency. She told her exactly what had happened with the client that morning. She spoke calmly and authoritatively. The woman listened, asked several questions and then apologised. She hadn't realised the client was treating staff like that, she said. She asked if Sylvie wanted to stay on their books. Thank you, but no, Sylvie said.

Someone had tried to call while she was talking to the agency. She pressed play on the answering machine. A familiar voice filled the hallway.

'Sylvie, it's Jill from Executive Stress Relief in Sydney calling. It's short notice, I know, but would you be free to meet me for lunch on Monday?' A soft laugh. 'In Melbourne, of course. I'm going to be down there for a couple of days. I'd love to meet up.' Brisk and to the point, as she always was.

Sylvie called back immediately. Jill had just gone into a meeting. Sylvie spoke to her assistant. Arrangements were made to meet at a French bistro at Southgate. Perfect. She couldn't wait. And the irony was if she hadn't been sacked from her first temp job in Melbourne, she wouldn't have been free to meet Jill.

She took off her horrible work pumps and did a stockinged-foot slide across the floor in celebration.

That night Sylvie spent an hour on Sebastian's computer, researching tips for successful dinner parties. Hers was all organised for the following Saturday. She'd rung and invited Max and Donald as well. They'd both accepted.

She'd decided on an Asian banquet. Several different starters and main courses, a symphony of taste sensations, according to the recipe books she'd consulted. She decided against a practice run. She knew how to cook, after all. And cooking with exotic ingredients was the same as cooking with ordinary ingredients. A matter of following steps, being organised, getting the timing right.

There were plenty of helpful websites. Sylvie soon had a list of tips on table settings, cocktails and serving etiquette, as well as possible witty conversation topics and after-dinner word games. She was about to log off when a bright sound heralded the arrival of an email. She clicked on it without thinking.

From: laurencedevereaux@hotmail.com
To: sebastiandevereaux@yahoo.com
Re: Dinner?

Seb, dinner Friday fortnight? Booking made. Will see you there unless I hear back to the contrary. Dad

She read it four times. At this exact moment, somewhere in Melbourne, her father was sitting at his computer. If she wanted to, she could write back immediately. Hi Dad, it's your daughter Sylvie. Long time no hear!

She was tempted, for one moment. Her fingers hovered over the keyboard. Then she disconnected and closed the computer down. She sent Sebastian a text telling him about the email, and apologising for opening it. That was all she needed to do with it.

8

'You're doing wonders for my social life, Sylvie,' Max said. 'Two nights out and an invitation to a dinner party. You're spoiling me.'

They were in the Spanish bar together again. Outside, the weather had turned bad, rain pelting down, the gutters rushing with water. Inside it was warm and cosy, the lights low, the background guitar music swirling around them. There were tapas plates and a nearly empty bottle of wine in front of them. The room was almost full, end-of-the-week chatter all around.

'You have Sebastian to thank, really,' she said. 'His dares, at least.'

'Am I that scary? That he had to dare you to ask me out?'

'Very scary.'

'How fantastic. I've been striking fear into the hearts of

people without being aware of it. Was it my latent masculinity? My powerful voice? My manly aura?'

'All those things, definitely.'

'Are you still scared?'

'Not any more.'

'So this is actually a date, not a drink? And I arrived here so innocently.'

'Not really.' Embarrassed, she backtracked. 'It was a dare to ask someone out on a date. Not you, specifically.' That sounded even worse. 'I didn't know anyone else to ask.' Worse still.

Max didn't seem hurt. 'I'm happy for you to practise on me. As long as I'm not ruining your chances with someone else. You haven't left anyone pining in Sydney?'

'You can't hear that howling? All the forlorn boyfriends I've left behind?' She shook her head. 'No, there's no one in Sydney.' A pause. 'And you?'

'No one in Sydney for me either. Or in Melbourne. Or in Adelaide, Perth, Hobart, Canberra, Brisbane or Darwin. There was a brief flirtation with someone in Wagga Wagga, or was it Coolangatta? Alas, it didn't work out between us. I'm footloose and fancy free. No, to be accurate, footloose, fancy free and scary.'

'I'm sorry to disappoint you, but you're really not scary at all.'

'I'm not? Good.' He smiled across the table at her.

Four hours later he was sitting close beside her, speaking into her ear. They were in a small jazz and blues club he liked, off Chapel Street in Prahran. The music was so loud it was the only way they could make themselves heard. She'd been telling him about Aunt Mill's phone calls.

'Are you actually keeping a record of these handy household hints?'

'I am, though I don't know what I'll do with them.' She'd told Max the ones she remembered. He said he was definitely going to try the linen and denture tablets tip.

'Mill's the one who asked you to be her companion?' he asked.

Sebastian had obviously told him everything. She nodded. 'She was housekeeper to this musician, Vincent Langan, and when he died he left —'

'Vincent Langan?' Max's shout coincided with the end of a song. Several people turned around. 'The jazz composer?'

'You've heard of him?'

'Of course I've heard of him. He was an absolute legend in the Sydney jazz scene in the fifties. Incredible. Completely underrated since. Did you actually know him?'

'I only met him once. At a family gathering.'

'Oh, God. I wouldn't have minded meeting him at a funeral. An abattoir open day. He didn't play anything that day, did he? Talk about his music?'

Sylvie shook her head.

Max made an elaborate show of touching her hand. 'I can't believe it. It's like that song, I danced with the girl who danced with the man who danced with the Prince of Wales.'

He laughed. 'Or however it goes. Wait till I tell my friends I've spent the evening with the woman whose great-aunt was the housekeeper to Vincent Langan.'

He was half-joking, Sylvie knew, but she suddenly sobered up. It was David all over again. Liked for her family, not for herself. She stood up. 'Max, I'm really sorry, but I need to head home. Can I get you a drink before I go?'

'Just like that? Are you okay?'

'A bad headache,' she lied. 'And toothache.'

'Headache and toothache? Together?'

It did sound suspicious. 'I'm prone to them unfortunately.'

'What did I say, Sylvie? I've upset you somehow.'

'Nothing. It's just a toothache. And headache.'

'Let me walk you home.'

'It's raining. I'll get a taxi.'

'If you're sure.'

'I'm sure.' She saw his expression change. He'd picked up every signal she was hurling at him. She was saying 'back away' and he was backing away. She felt a shimmer of regret. More than that. All evening she'd been finding him more and more attractive.

He became businesslike too. 'If you feel like calling off the dinner party, if your toothache is too bad —'

She'd forgotten all about the dinner party. She'd see that dare through, then the fun and games were over. 'Of course not,' she said, hating the false tone in her voice. 'I'll be fine once I get some painkillers. I'll see you next Saturday.'

'It was a great night tonight. Thanks a lot. I hope you feel better soon.'

'Thanks. See you.'

Ten minutes later, as she sat in the back of the taxi, rain pelting against the windows, she waited for the feeling of certainty to arrive, the knowledge that she'd made the right decision leaving when she did. That she'd been right to stand up for herself. Right not to let what happened with David happen again with Max.

The certainty didn't arrive. All that did was a sinking feeling she'd just spoilt something good.

It was a relief on Monday to be sitting with her old boss Jill over lunch. Familiar, businesslike. All that was different was they were in Melbourne, with the Yarra in the background instead of Sydney Harbour. Jill always ate in waterside restaurants. She told Sylvie the food tasted better.

Jill laughed as Sylvie told her of her first Melbourne temp experience.

'That will teach you to punch beneath your weight. What are you doing wasting your talents on data entry? You could have been running a place like that.'

'It's a deliberate approach. My slow takeover of Melbourne's office scene. Start at the bottom and work my way up.'

'Or you could start at the top.'

'Sorry?'

'You know I'm not one to mince my words, Sylvie. I'm not here on holiday. I'm here for business and to see you. Which is also business.'

Sylvie waited.

'An opportunity has come up for us to buy out an existing recruitment agency here. I want to start a Melbourne branch of Executive Stress Relief. Same principles, same philosophy, on a small scale to begin with. A sub-branch of the main recruitment business, if you like, targeting high-level clients. You know how it works. I want you to think about taking it on for me.'

'Managing it?'

'From day one. It would be your project.' Jill named an excellent salary. She mentioned a car. Rental assistance. An expense account.

'But why me?'

'You're the best person for the job. You've already proved yourself workwise, many times over. You also showed get up and go, moving down here the way you did.'

If only Jill knew. Sylvie kept her mouth shut.

'Will you think about it?' Jill said. 'I need an answer by the end of next week.'

'I'll definitely think about it.'

Jill held up her glass. 'To our business partnership?'

'To our business partnership,' Sylvie echoed.

9

Less than an hour into her dinner party, Sylvie knew she'd made a big mistake.

On the surface, all was perfect. The living room looked like the inside of a jewellery box. She'd turned the lights down low, sending a soft glow onto the golden drapes. Mellow background music was playing. She'd pushed the sofas to the edge of the room and moved the antique dining table and four chairs into the centre. With the food having an Asian theme, she'd set the table to match – serviettes folded into elegant origami swan shapes (she'd found the instructions on the Internet), chopsticks resting on elegant ceramic holders on a richly patterned tablecloth. Four low candles completed the look.

Throughout her preparations, she'd thought long and hard about Max and her reaction to his comments about Vincent

Langan. Her overreaction. Max had been paying for Evil David's sins, she realised. She hadn't been fair on him. He was obviously a genuine fan of Vincent Langan's music, and he'd had every right to be excited at the idea of Sylvie having met him. She'd decided to apologise to him as soon as she had the opportunity. And if he wanted it, she would give him Great-Aunt Mill's phone number. She knew Mill would love to talk about Vincent to anyone who cared to hear about him.

Max, Leila and Donald arrived within minutes of each other, just after seven-thirty. Sylvie had been dressed and made-up since before six-thirty, wearing a black top and cardigan, dark-orange skirt and her favourite high peep-toe shoes, which lifted her height to a towering five-foot four.

Her guests had dressed up too. Leila had wound her long red hair into a loose bun and made up her eyes in an exotic way. She was wearing a close-fitting red velvet vintage dress, showing lots of cleavage.

Donald was wearing a grey suit, white shirt and red tie, understated but elegant. He seemed at home in Sebastian's apartment, hanging up his coat, standing beside Sylvie and taking Max and Leila's coats as they arrived too. He'd kissed Sylvie's cheek as he came in. She'd wondered whether to say something, to whisper, 'I know about you and Sebastian and I heartily approve,' as she gave him a kiss back. She decided against it.

Max was wearing a dark-green smoking jacket over old-fashioned suit trousers. All borrowed from his flatmate's grandfather, he announced. 'I was thinking Gabriel Byrne in *Miller's Crossing*,' he said. 'But it's more bit-part-in-*Bugsy-Malone*, isn't it?'

Sylvie served champagne cocktails to begin. She felt like an actress in a 1940s comedy, laughing over her shoulder as she dropped sugar cubes into the tall glasses and the champagne fizzed and bubbled up the side of the glass. She'd been worried there would be awkward silences, but there wasn't a moment's lapse in conversation. Donald talked about a forthcoming author visit to his bookshop. It sparked a childhood anecdote from Leila about meeting her favourite writer and being sick on his shoes in excitement. Max told a story about a customer coming into the store, looking around and asking, 'Are these books for sale?'

Sylvie excused herself after serving another round of cocktails. Seb's kitchen was down a small hallway from the living room, not ideal for entertaining but she could still hear the conversations, at least. She'd banned them from coming into the kitchen. She didn't want anyone seeing her military-style preparations. Six of Sebastian's Asian cookbooks were arranged on the shelves. In front of each relevant recipe were the ingredients she needed. She had a running-order pinned on the wall beside the noticeboard.

The smells were glorious: spring onions, garlic, ginger, coriander, basil, sesame oil. She had spent nearly three hours at the Queen Vic food market, roaming the aisles, browsing the different stalls, revelling in having the time to do it. In Sydney, working full-time, it had been a matter of running into the nearest supermarket after work, grabbing whatever ingredients Fidelma was eating at the time and cooking them in simple ways – steaming, grilling or baking.

She wished she'd taken that approach now. Why hadn't she read the directions more clearly? Noticed each recipe had preparation times varying from thirty minutes to one hour, even if the cooking time in the wok was just a minute or two? How on earth did Chinese, Thai and Vietnamese restaurants manage to serve anybody, let alone so quickly? By having a team of cooks, of course. And more than one wok.

When in doubt, open another bottle of wine. 'Not long now,' she announced, putting another bottle of red on the table. They had already finished the first one.

They were halfway through the second bottle by the time she appeared with the starters: grilled prawns with coriander, lemongrass and ginger; and stir-fried calamari with garlic, celery and shallots. If they noticed the prawns were a little wan-looking from sitting in the oven keeping warm while she stir-fried the calamari, they didn't say. She was showered in compliments. If only the cooking ended there. She thought of the other ten bowls of ingredients waiting to be cooked for the main courses. Was it too late to order in a pizza?

The last prawn was on the plate, being argued over, when Donald's mobile rang. It was the security firm who monitored the bookshop. The alarm had been triggered. They'd checked, it looked secure, but they needed him to come down.

'I'll go,' Max said. 'You've worked back late all week.'

Donald was already folding his serviette. 'No. I don't pay you enough to do overtime. I'll take a look. I'll be back as soon as I can.'

He rang fifteen minutes later. There'd been an attempted break-in. The window into the storeroom was broken. He needed to wait for the glazier. 'I'm sorry, Sylvie.'

'It's fine. Do you want me to save some dinner for you? I can drop it around tomorrow.'

'That would be lovely.'

The evening changed from that moment. As Sylvie worked in the kitchen, chopping up more spring onions and garlic, measuring sesame oil, soy sauce and rice wine, she heard laughing. She heard Leila telling stories of disastrous auditions she'd done. Max saying she should forget about being a serious actor and turn her stories into a stand-up comedy routine. Leila laughingly dismissing him and telling another one.

Max saying, 'Seriously, why don't you think about it? I'll help you.'

'Help me?'

'Sure. Help you rehearse it. Stage it. There's open-mike spots in the comedy clubs all around town.'

'You're serious.'

'Deadly serious. Funny serious too.'

By the time Sylvie began bringing in the main course dishes (stir-fried mussels with black bean and chilli, crispy chicken in garlic-ginger sauce, and beef in spicy coconut milk), Max and

Leila had struck a mother lode of shared interests. Comedians they'd seen. Actors they admired. Plays they'd read. As Sylvie delivered the side dishes of rice and choy sum with oyster sauce, she realised she'd become a waitress in her own home.

They'd barely finished eating when Max said, 'One of the clubs off Chapel Street has a late-night stand-up slot.' He checked his watch. 'Starting in about half an hour.'

Sylvie knew it was up to her. If she insisted they stay, she'd feel guilty. She also knew it would take her a little while to prepare the dessert. Fresh fruit salad in cointreau, served with vanilla ice-cream. She hadn't cut up the fruit yet. She pulled a big smile from somewhere.

'What a fantastic idea,' she said. 'It was only going to be fruit for dessert. We could eat an apple each on the way.'

Max and Leila laughed uproariously. She realised she was about five glasses of wine behind them.

Within minutes of arriving at the comedy club, she knew she should have stayed home. In years to come, if she ever met Max and Leila's children, she would be able to tell them she was there the night they met and could report it had practically been love at first sight. They hadn't just hit it off. They'd slammed it off. There was so much electricity zipping back and forth between them Sylvie expected her hair to stand on end.

Neither of them seemed concerned when she made a show of looking at her watch at twelve-thirty. 'Do you mind if I head off?'

'Of course not.'

'You must be exhausted after all that cooking.'

'Thanks for a great night, Sylvie.'

'Really great. Fantastic food.'

She wondered if they'd even noticed what they were eating.

Leila gave her a flamboyant two-cheek kiss goodbye. Max hugged her. He felt good, as she'd expected he would. Something was missing, though. The promise of something. Whatever had been between them was gone, transferred in Leila's direction. She hadn't mentioned his comment about Vincent Langan, or apologised for her reaction. There seemed no reason to now. She suddenly felt stone-cold sober. Not only that. Foolish and sad as well.

They were both back engrossed in their conversation before she reached the exit.

The next morning Sylvie was woken by a knock at the door. She checked the bedside clock. Ten a.m. It was Leila. She looked like she'd been lit from inside. 'I know it's early, but I'm dying to talk. Can I come in?'

She was in and curled up on the sofa before Sylvie knew what had happened, like a cat on a wet winter evening.

'Sylvie, that was the best night ever. I have to thank you so much. Not only for dinner. But for —'

'Introducing you to Max?'

Leila put her arms around herself in a hug. 'I'm in love, Sylvie. I swear it. It's like we've known each other all our lives. He's so funny. So sweet. I can't believe I haven't met him before. Thank God you came down. If it wasn't for you, I —' Sylvie knew her expression had given her away when Leila suddenly clapped her hand over her mouth. 'Oh, God. Oh, God. There wasn't something between you, was there? And I've blundered in? Oh, Sylvie.'

'Of course not. I only just met him.' She was a better actress than Leila, she hoped. 'That's great you got on so well. So what did you get up to after I left?'

They'd stayed in the comedy club until it closed. Gone on to a late-night bar in the city centre. He'd walked her home at five a.m.

'And you're seeing him again?' Sylvie's voice was studiedly casual.

'Tonight. We were thinking about going for a drink. Or I might give him a call and see if he wants to go and see some more comedy.' A too-long pause. 'Would you like to come along?'

'No, I'm busy tonight, but thanks anyway.' A bright smile. 'So, can I get you a coffee?'

The first two dares were done. She rang Sebastian with her report.

'I did enjoy my date with Max, thank you very much. The

dinner party was pretty much a disaster, unfortunately. But I'm pleased to tell you your informal matchmaking plans worked a treat.'

'You and Max got together? Excellent!'

'Not me and Max. Max and Leila.'

'Max and *Leila*? Bloody hell.'

Sylvie had to laugh at the surprise in his voice. 'They've got a lot in common. Comedy, theatre . . .'

'I'm still surprised. I thought Leila would be too daft for Max. Shows how much I know.'

'She told me she's in love.'

'Leila falls in love every second week. Well, good luck to them, but I still think you were the better match. And you haven't finished the dares, by the way. Check the form. I want you to do one more for me.'

'Swim the length of the Yarra in a duck costume?'

'A little easier than that. I can't make dinner with Dad after all. I need you to go in my place.'

'Very funny.' Her heart started beating faster.

'Please, Sylvie. It would be bad manners if he turned up and I wasn't there.'

'Can't you ring and tell him you can't make it?'

'I think it's a good opportunity for you to meet him. And I want you to meet him.'

'More matchmaking? It hasn't worked out so far.' She hoped to deflect him with a joke. She also hoped he couldn't hear the note of panic in her voice.

'He's your father, Sylvie. He's not getting any younger. All I'm asking is that you have dinner with him. In return for letting you stay in my house rent-free. And yes, I know that's blackmail.'

'It's not blackmail, it's bullying.'

'I've been waiting for you to ask me for his contact number. I didn't want to force it on you. But not a word out of you about him. And I think it's important.'

'He's known I'm in Melbourne too. Have I had a message from him? An invitation to meet up? No.'

'Sylvie, he's got a lot on his plate. Complicated things. It's harder for him.'

She was surprised at her sudden anger. 'And it's easy for me?'

'Easier, yes. I think it is.' Silence for a moment. 'Please, Sylvie. Just go. And I don't think I should let him know it's you instead of me. If it's a surprise, he won't get too anxious beforehand —'

'He's had some sort of a breakdown? Is that what you're hinting at?'

'No, he hasn't had a breakdown. But all of this has been hard for him too. There's pride involved. Guilt. Try and understand.'

'How can I understand him? I don't know him.'

'So here's your chance. A starting point. A nice meal in a good restaurant, a couple of glasses of wine. It might be the best way to do it.'

Sylvie stayed silent. She pictured it. Pictured herself arriving at the restaurant. Seeing her father across the room. Walking over to him . . . Her heart started thumping again.

'Sylvie? Yes, no, or you'll think about it?'

'I'll think about it.'

Three times over the next few days she went to send an email to her father from Sebastian's address cancelling the dinner date. Three times she changed her mind. She distracted herself as best as possible. She visited the Art Gallery, Federation Square, the museums. She went on a walking tour through the city centre's laneways and back streets.

She spent hours thinking about Jill's offer. She tried to picture herself in the role, meeting with potential clients, networking, interviewing staff. To get into the right mood, she changed into her most formal clothes: jacket, skirt, the dreaded work shoes. She put on her pearl earrings. Make-up. She sat in front of the mirror.

'Good morning. My name is Sylvie Devereaux. I'm the manager of the newly established Melbourne branch of Executive Stress Relief, the fastest-growing recruitment agency in Australia. How may I help you?'

'Good afternoon. Thank you for coming to this presentation by Executive Stress Relief. My name is Sylvie Devereaux, manager of the Melbourne office, and I'm here to take the stress out of your staffing issues.'

'Thank you so much for our meeting, Mr Businessman. On behalf of Executive Stress Relief, I assure you I will do my utmost to provide you with professional and efficient staff-related services. Yes, despite our racy business name. And yes, I do insist you take your hand off my leg.'

She pulled a face into the mirror. 'For a good time, call Sylvie at Executive Stress Relief. Discretion assured.' Sebastian was right. It was a stupid name for a company.

She rang her mother. They talked about her painting, about the retreat, about Ray. Fidelma reported that Vanessa and Cleo had both decided to extend their holidays. Sylvie said she was enjoying Melbourne very much. She left it at that. She didn't mention her father or the job offer.

She had two messages from Max and Leila, inviting her to join them for dinner. Another night in a comedy club. She turned them down each time. Cupid didn't hang around after he shot his arrows either, did he? It was easier to think that than to give in to uncomfortable feelings of jealousy and disappointment.

The day before the dinner, she spent five minutes staring at her father's photograph. Was it too late? What would she say? What would he say? There was only one way to find out.

She texted Sebastian: Will meet Dad.

A one-word reply: Good.

*

Mill rang the afternoon of the dinner.

'Two quick tips, Sylvie. Coffee grounds make an excellent fertiliser for indoor plants. And a few drops of lemon juice will shine your shoes if you're out of polish. Now, tell me what's been happening with you in Melbourne.'

Sylvie told her about the dinner party, about the food, about Donald having to leave. She also told her about Max and Leila. About Sebastian's matchmaking plans going awry.

'Good on you for trying something adventurous with the cooking,' Mill said. 'I used to love entertaining too. Vincent's friends would come over at the drop of a hat. Starving, usually. They'd eat for hours, then play for hours. The nights we had, I can't tell you. As for the business with the young man, perhaps it wasn't your turn with him. People go through seasons, I think. Like dogs. Perhaps your female friend and your male friend were in the right season for each other. That's the way it works sometimes. Another time, you and he might have been in the right season together.'

Sylvie laughed. Mill's words helped, in a strange way. 'Have you ever thought about writing an agony aunt column?'

'No, who'd listen to me? You just need to accept it and move on, Sylvie. What else can you do – try and split them up? Get him back? Too late for that. Let it run its course. If he was meant for you, he'll find a way back. Now, what else is going on?'

Sylvie said it before she realised. 'I'm having dinner with my father tonight.'

'Heavens above. Does your mother know?'

'No.'

'Don't tell her, for God's sake. She'll have kittens.'

Sylvie nearly laughed again. Her great-aunt had a way of defusing situations without realising. 'Mill, did you know him?'

'I met him a few times. And I was at their wedding, of course. What a grand affair that was.'

'What was he like back then?'

'Handsome. Talented. Absolutely mad about your mother in the early days.'

'Why did it go so wrong between them?'

'There were rumours, but whoever knows what goes on between two people.'

Sylvie didn't want discretion. 'What did you hear?'

Mill was quiet for a moment. 'I don't know what was gossip and what was truth. I heard talk of money worries. And Fidelma's a handful, of course. She always was, even as a child. An artist, you see. They're difficult. You should know – you've lived and worked with four of them, five, counting your father, I suppose. I don't like those sisters of yours, by the way. Very stuck-up. Talented, yes. But extremely unlikable.'

'They're artists. They behave differently. It comes with the territory. I know because I'm not artistic. I'm the boring one of the family. The square peg.'

'You are having a pity party today. Swimming in a sea of woe-is-me. Don't be silly. You can't have everyone in a family being an artist. And thank God for that. It would be an unworkable situation. Artists need support. They're helpless on their own. Painters, for example. They need gallery owners, framers, paint manufacturers. People to look at their work. Patrons. Look at Vincent van Gogh – helpless without his brother Theo. Musicians are the same – nothing on their own. I'm speaking from experience, of course. They need constant reassurance. Audiences. People to make their instruments. Build stages. Sell tickets. It's the same with writers. They need readers, booksellers, publishers, printers . . . Even comedians need people to laugh at their jokes. Try to look at it that way, Sylvie. Maybe your mother and your father and your sisters and your brother are the square pegs, the odd ones out. So needy. So fragile. In fact, I'd say they are. I've never met an artist who isn't odd, have you?'

'No.'

'Exactly. You're much better off being the person you are. Independent. Self-sufficient. Sane. Let them be the odd ones out and you can be the odd one in. Now, I must go. George is about to arrive and I promised I'd serve him a Harvey Wallbanger for cocktail hour tonight. Bye for now. Enjoy dinner with your father.'

10

Sylvie chose simple clothes. A pale-green T-shirt, a dark-green skirt. She put several sparkling clips in her hair, applied more make-up than usual, looked at herself for a long moment, then washed off the make-up and took out the clips. She wasn't glamorous like Vanessa or Cleo. There was no point pretending otherwise. If she disappointed him, there was little she could do.

Sebastian had been concerned about their father getting anxious. Sylvie's own blood pressure was heading skywards. This wasn't just a dinner. If she had been worried about life in Melbourne reaching childhood expectations, it had nothing on her expectations about her father.

She wanted to meet him. She needed to meet him. She was glad Sebastian had forced the issue. Because there was no way she would have dared do it herself. There was too much that could go wrong. She tried to keep perspective. They wouldn't run into each other's arms, like the scene in the final chapter of *The Railway Children* which always brought her to tears. Bobbie on the station platform, seeing her father for the first time in many hard months.

Sylvie knew the whole scene word for word:

'"Oh! my Daddy, my Daddy!" That scream went like a knife into the heart of everyone in the train, and people put their heads out of the windows to see a tall pale man with lips set in a thin close line, and a little girl clinging to him with arms and legs, while his arms went tightly round her.'

Sylvie didn't know if she and her father would even touch each other. She could feel the young, hurt version of herself nestling deep inside still, the little girl who hadn't received any birthday cards or phone calls for many years. The same girl who had slowly and methodically sealed off the part of her mind that wanted to think about her father, who missed him. Who would like to have talked to him over the years.

Would they manage any of those conversations tonight? Manage to catch up on even one year of her life, let alone twenty-one? She wanted to, she realised. She looked in the mirror one more time before she left the apartment. 'Hello, Laurence,' she said to her reflection. 'I'm Sylvie, your daughter.'

She easily found the Malaysian restaurant. She had walked past it many times the last fortnight. There were about a dozen tables, half of them full. Before she had a chance to look around, the waitress came over and greeted her.

'Good evening. Do you have a booking?'

'I'm meeting someone.'

'Name?'

'Devereaux.'

The elderly man at the table by the window looked up. He was wearing a jumper that looked like it had seen better days. There was a jug of water in front of him. She looked closer. Curly hair. Enquiring eyes.

He said her name first. 'Sylvie?' He stood up. 'It's Sylvie?'

'Hello.' She stepped towards him. 'Sebastian couldn't make it. I came in his place.'

He was looking intently at her. 'I've seen photographs, of course, but they don't do you justice. You're lovely. You're like your grandmother.'

She gazed back at him. It was like time-lapse photography. The handsome man in the photos worn down by age, battered by life.

'Please, sit down,' he said.

There was so much to say she didn't know how to start. She watched him fidget with a napkin. All day she had rehearsed conversations in her head with him. Now her mind was blank.

He looked as uncomfortable as she was feeling. 'I'm sorry. I don't know where to start with chit-chat.'

'I'm not good at chit-chat either.'

He gave a brief smile. 'I've brought a couple of books. We could sit here and read if you like. Or I've got the crossword.'

It was a cryptic one, she noticed. 'Are you good at them?'

'Not bad.'

The waitress arrived with menus and a wine list. Two other groups of people arrived, taking tables behind and beside them. Sylvie felt very self-conscious. This hadn't been a good idea. A first meeting in twenty-one years in a public place like this?

Her father picked up the menu. She picked up hers. There was silence while they both read.

She looked up at the sound of a chair being pushed back. His chair.

He was standing up. 'Sylvie, I'm sorry. I can't stay.' His hands were shaking.

'But —'

'I'm sorry.'

She could only watch as he walked quickly across the room and out the door.

She sat for a few minutes. She couldn't follow him. Wouldn't follow him. She politely told the waitress she needed more time.

'The gentleman?'

'He got called away.'

The second time the waitress came, Sylvie apologised and said unfortunately she needed to leave too. Her shock had turned to anger. As she walked out, the waitress gave her a puzzled look.

Sebastian rang her on her mobile before she had a chance to dial his number. 'Are you okay?'

'How do you know?'

'He rang me. From a phone box up the street, by the sound of things.'

Sylvie glanced around, expecting to see him. No sign. 'What the hell is going on, Seb? What games are you both playing with me?'

'Sylvie, it's not games, I promise you. I'm so sorry it's happened like this. But it's not something I think I should explain on the phone. Are you free tomorrow night?'

'Yes, but —'

'I'll ask for a night off. Come back to Melbourne and take you out to dinner. The same place. You'll like it. And you may even get to eat something this time.'

She knew he was trying to cheer her up, but it didn't feel funny. None of this did. She agreed on a meeting time, then abruptly finished the call.

She walked home, down Toorak Road, onto Punt Road, hardly noticing her surroundings. Was that it? That was her big reunion with her father? Their first conversation after all those years? She didn't know if she wanted to cry or rage or even laugh. She was completely confused. If anyone had the right to storm out, surely it was her? She was the one who had been abandoned.

She took out her phone again and pressed speed dial. She didn't waste time with a greeting. 'Seb, I need Dad's number. His address.'

'No, Sylvie. Not yet. After we've met.'

'Forget this. Stop trying to control me. You were at me because I didn't ask you for his details and now I want them you won't give them to me?'

'I made a mistake. I thought things would be different.'

'You thought he might stay long enough to have a glass of wine, you mean? A starter? A prawn cracker or two?' She took a ragged breath. 'What did I do wrong, Seb?'

'You didn't do anything. You couldn't have done anything.'

'What is it? You have to tell me.'

'Sylvie, I can't, not over the phone. It's a long story and I'm about to get called back to the set. It's not fair to you or him.'

'I'll go to the university tomorrow to see him, then.'

'He doesn't work there any more.'

'Then I'll go to his home. I'll look him up in the phone book.'

'He's not in the phone book.'

'Who is he? The Scarlet Pimpernel?'

'Sylvie, please. One more day. I'll be there tomorrow night. Before seven, I promise. Will you wait till then?'

It didn't look like she had any choice. 'Okay.'

'I'm sorry, Sylvie. I hoped it would be different. I made a big mistake.'

'It's not your mistake, Seb.'

'It's not yours, either. Remember that.'

*

There was no message from Mill waiting on the answering machine when she got home. There was, however, an email. Addressed to Sebastian, written to her.

Sylvie, I'm sorry. I hope Sebastian will explain things better than I can. LD

He hadn't even signed it Dad.

The next day stretched out too long and too lonely in front of her. She waited until nine and then phoned the other temp agencies she'd contacted. Whatever job was going, she'd take.

One hour later, she was in the boardroom of a fifteenth-floor office on Collins Street, surrounded by three thousand envelopes, address labels and circulars.

The young woman who'd met her at reception was apologetic. 'It's completely mindless work, I'm sorry. Just stuffing envelopes. I can get you a radio if you'd like one. And please take all the coffee breaks you need. You'll go crazy otherwise.'

'I'll be fine,' Sylvie said. 'It's perfect. Thanks very much.'

She was waiting in the restaurant when Sebastian arrived at ten to seven that night. He was carrying his bag and a laptop over his shoulder. He'd obviously come directly to the restaurant without going home first. It had been less than a fortnight since she'd seen him, but she nearly cried with the relief. He came straight over and gave her a hug.

'You okay, Sylvie?'

'Not really. How are you?'

'Work, good. Social life, good. Sister, worried about her. Brother, guilty he landed her in it.'

'What is it, Seb? Is he sick? Dying?'

'No quicker than any of us.' He glanced around for the waitress. 'Would you like a drink before we start? I'm presuming you didn't get a glass of wine with Dad last night?'

'He's an alcoholic. A drug addict. His life's a mess. That's what you're saying.'

'He's a mess, yes. But he's not an alcoholic. Or a drug addict. Not exactly.'

He wouldn't say more until they had ordered and a bottle of red wine was in front of them.

'Tell me everything, Seb. Don't leave anything out. Don't feel you have to protect me.'

'I don't any more.' He poured their wine. 'I'm driving you crazy waiting, I know, but I'm also proving a point. Good parts of life go on even when there are bad things in the background.'

'Nice philosophy, but would you please just tell me?'

'Dad's a disaster area, Sylvie. Broke. Almost on the streets. He has been for years.'

She stared at him. 'You're making that up.'

He shook his head. 'He's got a gambling addiction. Not just an addiction. A curse. He's been ruined by it. He can't beat it.'

'Gambling? Horseracing? Poker?'

'Horses, dogs, cats probably. Cards. Sporting matches. You name it, he's gambled on it. He's been like it on and off all his life.'

'But how can he be a gambling addict? He's an academic. A poet.'

'That's got nothing to do with it. In any case, he hasn't worked at the university for sixteen years. He hasn't written poetry for years. Or if he has, he hasn't had anything published.'

Sylvie was having trouble taking it all in. 'Why didn't you tell me any of this before now?'

'He asked me not to. And I didn't want to. You felt bad enough about him as it was.'

'Then why didn't you tell me before I met him last night?'

'I should have, I know that now. But I didn't know what phase he'd be in. It's like alcoholism. He lasts weeks without gambling and then it's like a fever, it's all he does, all he thinks about, and bam, all the money's gone. He's been good the past few times I've seen him. I hoped he was still like that. That you'd get on okay, at least have a meal, a conversation with him before you learned about the whole situation. Did he have a jug of water in front of him when you arrived?'

Sylvie nodded.

'That means he's bad again. It's a kind of signal he has, to tell me I'll have to pay for dinner. If I arrive and he has a bottle of wine on the table, it's his shout. It's his way of telling me without telling me.'

'When did you find all this out? When you moved down here with him?'

He nodded. 'The giveaway was when the TV kept going missing. When the fridge stayed empty for weeks on end. When I realised if I wanted to study I'd have to find the fees myself.'

'But you never said anything. All those times you came up on visits. Why didn't you tell us? Tell me?'

'What was the point? Mum hated him anyway. Vanessa and Cleo had decided he was public enemy number one. And Mum wouldn't let you see him, in any case.' He paused. 'Do you wish I had told you before now?'

She thought about it. What would it have changed? She slowly shook her head. 'Seb, was it terrible? Has it been terrible for you all these years?'

'Sometimes, yes. Most of the time, it's sad but it's not terrible. It was harder for Mum than anyone, I think. You know he sold most of her family heirlooms before she realised what was going on?'

'The paintings? The lamps? That's where they went?'

He nodded. 'All sold to pay back debts. Nothing much has changed since then. He owns some clothes, a few books – that's about it. His house is practically a slum as well, but it's the best he can do. He gets a pension these days, but it's touch-and-go sometimes.'

'So he's always been like this?'

'It was in his blood, I think. His father was a bookie, did you know that?'

Sylvie shook her head. She knew hardly anything about her father.

'Dad said it started with cards for him. Playing poker with friends, games that turned into night-long sessions. Small bets that turned into big bets. From what he's told me, he was up to his neck in debts before he knew it.'

'And Mum always knew?'

'You don't remember them fighting about it?'

Sylvie remembered fights, but not what they'd been about. She'd always run to her room when they started shouting at each other.

'Any time they had any money, he spent it. Or took it. Mum had to kick him out or there would have been nothing left, I'm sure of it. I take my hat off to her. She's always been away with the fairies, but she did bring you all up. She's a shrewd businesswoman under all those silk scarves.'

'So after they divorced, Dad didn't help her financially?'

Sebastian laughed. 'Oh, he might have sent her the odd five-dollar note now and then. When he wasn't on a poker binge or a greyhound binge or a horseracing binge.'

'But what about you, Seb? Who paid for your food and the rent and all of that?'

'I learned to steal too. Don't look so shocked. I stole from him. Out of his wallet, whenever I knew he had any money. I kept it hidden so we had enough to pay bills, buy food, cover the rent. Until I decided enough was enough and I moved out of there.'

'Did it make you hate him?'

Sebastian shook his head. 'He can't help it. No, that's not true. Sometimes he can and sometimes he can't. But put it this way, I learned at a young age never to say "Want to bet on it?" to him.'

They laughed a little at that.

'Is that why you moved out so young?' Sebastian had just turned eighteen when he got a flat on his own, she remembered.

'Part of the reason. I knew that if I stayed, I'd be forever bailing him out. I'd done enough of that. And that wasn't doing either of us any good. Especially after he lost his job. He kept skipping lectures to go to the bookies. It took a while, but eventually I realised it wasn't my job to take care of him.'

'Seb, I'm so sorry. I wish I'd known. For you, if not him.'

'I was okay, Sylvie. Really. I got mad sometimes, and then I'd get sad. It's the same now. But I still enjoy him. When he's in good form – pardon the racing pun – he's good company. He still reads a lot, still thinks. But I'm not in charge of his life, and he's not in charge of mine.'

'This is why he never got in contact with us, isn't it?'

'Most of the reason.' He was quiet for a moment. 'I've

thought a lot about it, talked to people about it —'

'Therapy, you mean?'

'Nothing so interesting. I went to Gam-Anon. For families of gamblers. I didn't like what I heard, but it made me understand there was nothing I could do about it. It suited Dad to live separately from me. It suited him to live separately from all of us. No Fidelma on his back, no kids to feel responsible for. Out of sight, out of mind, out of guilt.'

She felt tears well and blinked them away. 'I wanted to like him. I thought he would be the missing piece in my life. That meeting him would make everything right. And . . .'

Sebastian waited.

'I didn't feel anything. He was just an old man. An old man who got up and left in the middle of dinner.'

'Not the middle. You didn't even get started, did you? Talk about a cheap date.'

She couldn't laugh. She was still too angry. Too hurt. 'What do I do now, Seb? Do I meet him again? Do I have to get to know him? Do I have to love him?'

'You have to do whatever feels right. But how can you love him yet? You don't know him.'

'He's my father. I'm supposed to love him, aren't I?'

'I don't think there are rules about that. If there are, he's broken a few of them. So I'd say you're even on that score.'

'Do you love him?'

'I like him. I feel sorry for him. I care what happens to him. Is that love? I don't know.'

During dinner Sebastian told her more stories of life with their father. Her eyes filled with tears again.

He noticed. 'Don't cry for me, Sylvie. Seriously. I still think I got the better end of the deal. You're the one who had to live with Fidelma and Heckle and Jeckle.'

'I wish I'd known. I wish I could have helped you.'

'There was no help to be done. And you know now.'

'Better late than never?'

'Exactly.'

Over coffee, she told him about the job offer from Jill. He was delighted for her. 'But you don't look too pleased.' He hesitated. 'It's not because of Dad being here in Melbourne, is it? Knowing about him? Has it ruined things?'

'No.' She thought about it. 'No, it hasn't. I'm still trying to work it all out. Whether I should take it. Where I would live. How I would live.'

'Of course you should take it. And the rest is simple. You'd live with me until you found your own place. My friends would be your friends. It's all here waiting for you, Sylvie. Your new life, waiting to be lived. Come on, get that sad look off your face. It's not the end of the world with Dad, I promise you. He's not the devil, or evil. He's just a mess. But it's his life, and he's living it the way he wants to. And we have to live our lives too.'

'I think I wanted a happy ending, Seb. I wanted it to all work out differently.'

'You're not at the end yet. Who knows how it will be between you? Give him some time. And give yourself some time as well. And try not to expect too much. He's only human. And so are you.'

'It's not that simple, is it?'

'I've had twenty years to think about it, Sylvie. It actually is that simple. Not easy, but simple.' He reached across and touched her hand. 'Trust me. I'm your big brother.'

11

They left the restaurant straight after their meal. No visits to bars or late-night clubs. Sylvie helped Sebastian carry his bags up the stairs to his apartment. He was staying just the one night, returning to the film set the next morning.

'There'll be a message from Mill,' she said over her shoulder. 'She's started ringing each night with one of her handy household tips.'

'She has? I'm changing the number first thing tomorrow.'

The light was flashing. Sylvie smiled. 'Told you.' She pressed the button.

'Sylvie, it's Mill.' Her voice sounded odd. 'I need some help. I've a pain in my chest. I've rung my neighbours but they're out. I didn't want to make a fuss and ring the doctor but . . . it's a sharp pain. You're not there. I'll try —'

Sylvie exchanged an alarmed glance with Sebastian. She

replayed the message.

'It's not a joke, is it?' Sebastian asked.

'She doesn't make those kinds of jokes.' Sylvie picked up the phone and rang Mill's number. There was no answer. She tried again. It rang out one more time.

She didn't hesitate. She dialled 000 and quickly explained.

'We can send someone around,' the operator said. 'What's the address?'

She didn't know. She'd never been to Vincent's house. 'It's a terrace in Surry Hills.'

'Miss, we can't help without an address. Can you find it out? Call us back?'

Sebastian rang Fidelma's number on the landline. He got the answering machine. Sylvie rang Cleo and Vanessa on their mobiles. She got their voicemail in both cases.

At Sylvie's suggestion, Sebastian logged onto the web and googled Vincent Langan's name. 'No good,' he called. 'It just says he lived in Surry Hills.'

Sylvie had a brainwave. 'Seb, quick, get the website for George's Gorgeous Gardens. He knows where she lives.'

George answered his mobile immediately. Sylvie urgently explained.

'I live just three streets away,' he said. 'I'll call the ambulance and go there right now myself. I've got a key.'

'Will you call me back?'

'As soon as I can.'

*

George rang back thirty minutes later. Mill was on her way to hospital. He'd found her unconscious on her living-room floor. She'd had a heart attack.

'She's got a heart condition?'

'It's usually under control with tablets. But she's been so busy getting Vincent's house organised, she wasn't taking care of herself. But she'll be okay. She said it, the doctor said it. She also told me to give you a tip from her.'

'A tip? At a time like this?'

There was amusement in his voice. 'She said it was a simple one. "Never forget to take your medication."'

Sylvie awoke at seven the next morning. Sebastian was still asleep, his bedroom door shut. She dressed quietly and walked out into the misty morning.

She loved autumn in Melbourne. It felt different to autumn in Sydney. She felt closer to nature, though it did help living next to the Botanic Gardens. She walked around the boundary of the gardens, listening to the traffic, the pounding feet of the joggers, snatches of conversation. She thought of the different parts of the city she had visited. All there was still to be uncovered. The possibility of getting to know her father better, if he let her and if she decided she wanted to.

There were great opportunities for her, she could feel it. Different work, a new share-house, the distance she needed from her mother and sisters, the fun she would have with

Sebastian. She got the feeling again. Of anticipation. Knowing she could take charge of her own life.

Sebastian was coming out of the bathroom in his dressing-gown when she let herself in.

'You've been to get me fresh croissants and orange juice. What a thoughtful sister.'

'I haven't but I can.'

'I don't eat breakfast. Make me coffee, though, and you'll be in my good books all day.'

She had a tray of coffee waiting on the table beside the bay window when he came back from getting dressed. She poured them both a cup and then sat down opposite him.

'You look serious,' he said.

'I am.' It was the right thing to do. She knew it. 'Seb, I've decided something.'

'What?'

'I'm going back to Sydney. I was offered a job before I came down here. I'm going to take it.'

'What job? With the agency?'

She shook her head. 'As Mill's companion.'

He burst out laughing. 'That's a cracker, Sylvie. Bedpans. Tablets. Oh yes, you'll be really happy.' He stopped and looked at her. 'Oh, my God. You're serious.'

She nodded.

'But what about the big Melbourne job?'

'I don't want it.'

'You'd be so good at it.'

'It's not what I want to do. I feel like I've done work like it already. Long hours. Stressful demands. It wouldn't feel new.'

'But Melbourne would be new. There's so much here.'

'I'll come down more often. See you more regularly.'

'It's not because of Dad, is it?'

'No.' She was sure of that. 'I wanted him to be different. I wanted him to want to get to know me. But that won't change whether I'm here or in Sydney, will it?'

Sebastian shook his head. 'No, I don't think so. But Sylvie, talk about frying pan into the fire. You're a young woman. Mill's an old, mad woman.'

'She's not. She's only in her seventies and she's not mad. Eccentric, but not mad. Did you know she was Vincent Langan's lover for forty years? That he was one of the best jazz musicians of his age? That what she doesn't know about household tips isn't worth knowing? That she has lived through a world war? That she cooked dinner for every jazz and blues singer worth their note in Sydney in the fifties and sixties? She's full of stories. She's funny. I like her.'

'So ring her once a week. Become penpals. Why do you have to go and live with her?'

'I want to get to know her while there's still time. And she needs a hand getting her affairs in order.'

'More affairs? A woman of her age?'

'Her paperwork. She's got boxes of recipes and tips. All of Vincent's papers and his music collection. I'd like to help her with them.'

'You are serious, aren't you?' He laughed ruefully. 'Where did I go so terribly wrong?'

'You didn't go wrong. You went right. You showed me another way of living. A different way. And I realised this morning I liked the old way. I just needed to come at it from a different direction.'

'So you're moving back home?'

She shook her head. 'I'm moving into an upstairs room in Mill's house. It's painted blue and it looks out on a fig tree.'

'How do you know?'

'She told me.'

'But what if I said I want you to stay here with me?'

An echo. She thought of herself as a child. *I want to be with my brother.*

'If you still want me when we are old and grey, I'll come and be your housekeeper. I just need to pick up all the tips from Mill first.'

'Not the racy ones. I don't want some slapper of a house-keeper living with me, bringing home elderly gents from the local bowls club.'

'I promise. No elderly gents.'

'Are you sure, Sylvie?'

'About the elderly gents? Yes, positive.'

'Not them.'

She smiled. 'I am sure, Seb. I'm absolutely sure.' She said it in a crisp English accent.

He grinned at her. 'Then come here and give your poor lonely brother a big hug. Your poor lonely abandoned brother.'

'That's emotional blackmail, isn't it?'

He leaned back and raised his eyes to the ceiling. 'She recognises it at last. My work here has not been in vain. Go forth, young Sylvie. You have my blessing.'

They hugged on it.

One week later, she had a farewell night out with Sebastian, Donald, Leila and Max. Dinner, drinks, lots of laughing. She was very aware of Leila and Max, still in the early stages of their relationship, all glances and touching. She felt pangs of regret, mixed up with jealousy, uncomfortable feelings. She made a conscious effort to seem relaxed and pleased for them both.

Sebastian was the life of the party, bemoaning the fact she was leaving, making fun of her. 'My plan went awry. I had it all sorted. Sylvie rents my spare room and cooks all my dinners, works part-time in Donald's bookshop and forms a long and lasting relationship with you, Max.'

Max shrugged, putting on a sad expression. 'She wasn't interested in me, I'm afraid. Obviously too used to those Flash Harry Sydney types. Still, I was able to drown my sorrows with Leila.'

'Stop that, you,' Leila said, with a too-loud giggle. 'Our meeting was fate and you know it.' She planted a big kiss on his cheek.

Sylvie kept a bright smile on her face, laughing with every-one else. Is that what Max had thought? That she hadn't shown any interest? Would everything have been different if she hadn't left the music club that night? Not taken offence at his curiosity about Vincent Langan? Would Leila still have knocked him off his feet? She was glad when Donald engaged her in conversation and she could turn away from Max and Leila.

The party ended soon after. Leila gave her a big farewell hug. 'I'll ring you, Sylvie. Every week, I promise. We can be long-distance friends.'

'I'd like that.' She meant it too.

Donald hugged her as well. 'Good luck, Sylvie. See you soon, I hope.'

'I hope so too,' she said.

Max was next. 'I hope Sydney treats you well. Keep in touch.'

'I will. You too.' She wondered if they would. She hugged him then pulled away first, for her own sake. He still felt good. Tall and solid. But out of her reach.

She arrived back in Sydney on the two-thirty flight. She'd rung Fidelma and told her the news. Fidelma said it all sounded like a marvellous idea. She then told Sylvie about her plans for her new exhibition opening. Flame throwers, she was thinking, to tie in with the idea of the elements. Sylvie said she thought it sounded wonderful and gave her the name of two excellent event organisers. Fidelma didn't offer to collect her from the airport and Sylvie didn't ask. She was nearly thirty. She was perfectly capable of getting a taxi or a bus home. To her new home.

Mill had rung the night before to tell her once more how pleased she was at Sylvie's decision. She'd been out of the hospital for four days. She was fighting fit again, she said.

'We'll set some ground rules too, I promise. You're not coming to be my nurse. Or my companion, really, now I think about it. We can be partners. How does that sound?'

Sylvie thought it sounded good.

As she came out into the arrivals area, a man in his mid-thirties came up to her. Medium height, brown-faced, dressed in faded jeans and a long-sleeved T-shirt pushed up over muscled arms.

'Sylvie?' At her nod, he put out his hand. 'I'm George. Your aunt's gardener. She asked me to come and collect you.'

He had a smiling, open face. She found herself smiling back at him. 'How did you know it was me?'

He picked up her case as if it was a matchbox. 'She said you were small and lovely. And you are. Come on, the car's this way.'

EPILOGUE

One year later

Sylvie and Mill were sitting on the swinging chair on the verandah, sipping from cocktail glasses. It had been a warm autumn day with sunshine and blue sky. Through the open French doors they could clearly see the TV set. On screen a bride and groom were dancing. The footage was shaky, as if filmed by an amateur. As the couple did a twirl, the husband tripped and went flying across the dance floor into the wedding cake. The footage ran forwards and backwards, all with a comical musical soundtrack.

The host appeared on screen, a backdrop of the groom with wedding cake all over him behind her. It was Leila. She put her hands on her hips and gave a big laugh. 'That's what I call trying to have your cake and eat it too! That's it for tonight. Please keep your videos coming in. Don't forget, if Calamity Calls, call me! Goodnight!'

As soon as the credits had rolled, Sylvie picked up the phone beside her and rang a Melbourne number. 'It was fantastic, congratulations.'

'You think?' Leila said. 'I've been hiding under the bed since I recorded it last week.'

'You're a natural.'

'What did Mill think?'

'Mill, what did you think?'

'A little ripper.'

Sylvie and Leila had kept in contact since Sylvie left Melbourne. Leila's career had got a sudden boost six months previously with her appearance on a fledgling comedy show on one of the community stations. A TV scout for one of the bigger networks had seen her. She was edgy and kooky, apparently. Just what he needed for the host of a new show of video bloopers from around the world. Each program would begin with a monologue from Leila talking about her latest catastrophe. She had no problem finding material, she told Sylvie.

Her relationship with Max had lasted only two months. A mutual decision. 'I'm not surprised,' Leila had said. 'Why should my love-life be any less disastrous than the rest of my life? At least we're still on speaking terms. My last boyfriend nearly took out a contract on me.'

Leila had been up to stay with Sylvie and Mill twice. She loved the house. 'It would make me want to take up jazz,' she said the first time. 'How long will the students get to stay here?'

'A year, but then we'll help them find other accommodation,' Sylvie explained.

Her sister Cleo had been disgusted. 'Wasting a beautiful house on scholarship students? Mill should sell it and move out into the suburbs. What a waste of money.'

'It was in Vincent's will,' Sylvie explained for the third time. 'He wanted Mill to use her inheritance to further jazz studies.'

'Couldn't she have bought a few CDs and given them to a university?'

'Vincent was from the country,' Mill had explained to Sylvie in her first week back in Sydney. 'He wanted me to do something to help other young musicians.'

It had been Sylvie's idea to turn the house into a home away from home for music students. Establish a trust that would continue long after Mill, or indeed Sylvie herself, had died. To also use Vincent's healthy royalties to fund three scholarships.

Vanessa was just as horrified. 'So you have to live with her and be her glorified secretary with no promise of a hefty inheritance at the end of it? You're mad.'

Twelve months earlier Sylvie had known nothing about jazz, or composing, or the difficulties young musicians faced. Now, she couldn't say she was an expert, but she was definitely a fan. The house was filled with music, talk of music, music magazines. At the moment, there were three students living with her and Mill. A piano player from the Hunter Valley, a trumpet player from Alice Springs and a double bass player from Perth.

There were great plans for the future, too. Open days twice a year, so visitors could stroll through the house, learn about Vincent's career, look at original sheet music, hear old recordings and read about the jazz scene in Sydney from the late 1950s onwards.

Sylvie was busy five days a week. Every day was different. Mill was the ideas person, but she left most of the work to Sylvie. It worked best that way, they'd discovered. And lately, Mill had been otherwise occupied.

Sylvie had dropped a collection of her tips into the local free newspaper. Since then, Mill had been contributing a fortnightly 'Ask Mill' column. She read each letter that was sent in and spent some time drafting her replies. The questions had been about cooking and housekeeping to begin with. These days, most of the hundred or so letters she received each week were about relationship problems. A producer from one of the radio stations who lived locally had read several of the columns and invited Mill on to his show. She had unfortunately sworn in the first broadcast, but once the fuss died down (there'd been twenty calls of complaint, apparently), he hoped to bring her back for another show.

'He'd better hurry up before I die,' was all Mill said about it.

In Melbourne, Sebastian and Donald were still together, still happy. She heard snippets of news about Max from Sebastian.

He wasn't working in the bookshop any more. He had been offered work with a touring comedy production. It had come to Sydney but Sylvie had been away with Fidelma at the retreat that week. She went away with her mother every few months. It always coincided with Ray's visits to see his children from a previous marriage. Sylvie preferred it that way.

She sent the occasional email to her father. He sent the occasional one back. So far they had written only about books they'd read and films they'd seen. Each sentence seemed heavy with other meaning, but Sylvie didn't know where to start and didn't know if her father wanted her to. Fidelma still hadn't asked about him. Sylvie hadn't mentioned him either. She had reached no firm decisions or conclusions about him, or her feelings for him. She was taking Sebastian's advice, going slowly and letting it unfold in a way they both could cope with. No happy ending, but the best they could do.

'So have you seen Max yet?' Leila asked now on the phone.

'Max? Seen him where?'

'There. He's in Sydney. He got a one-year contract with the Sydney Theatre Company. I gave him your number last month. We caught up for a drink before he left. He said he was going to call.'

'No, he hasn't.' The sudden pang surprised her.

'I've got his number if you want it.'

'Sure,' she said, sounding as casual as she could, while her heart started beating faster. She took down the number.

Beside her Mill was making a show of looking at her watch. They were due over at Gorgeous George's house for dinner. It was apparently to celebrate his third child's fifth birthday, but Sylvie knew it was any excuse for a party. George and his wife Sarah had become Sylvie's good friends in the past twelve months. They had hit it off immediately, from the moment George picked her up at the airport.

She said a quick goodbye and another congratulations to Leila, then hung up. Mill had her eyes shut, head leaning back against the verandah rail, the near-empty cocktail glass in her hand. Mill was taking lots of catnaps these days. Not surprising, she was seventy-four years old. And working hard for a woman of her age.

'Mill?' Sylvie asked.

'Mmm?'

'There hasn't been a call for me recently that you forgot to pass on, has there?'

'Man or woman? Friend or foe? Family or non-family?'

'Man. Friend. Non-family. Called Max.'

'Now I think of it, yes. Last week.'

'What did he say?'

'Asked to speak to you.'

'What did you say?'

'Said you weren't home.'

'Was I?'

'Nope.'

'Did you forget to tell me or decide not to tell me?'

'It never hurts a man to have to do a bit of running after his prey.'

'I'm not Max's prey and you know it's rude not to pass on messages.'

'You've got his number now, haven't you?'

'Were you eavesdropping then?'

'Of course. That's why I got the hearing aid installed. So I could hear.'

They took simultaneous sips from their cocktail glasses.

'Mill, can I ask for a tip?'

'Ask away.'

'If you had met someone and thought that something might happen between you but before it did, something happened to make it impossible, but then it looked like you had a chance to make something happen, what would you do?'

'I'd ring him,' Mill said. 'Declare your intentions. Show your interest. As soon as possible.'

'Now, you mean?'

'Now,' Mill said. 'Before we go to Gorgeous George's.'

Sylvie went inside to make the call. He answered on the fifth ring.

'Max?'

'Sylvie?'

This time she didn't want to make a mess of it. She wanted to be clear. 'Max, I'm sorry to launch into it even before we catch up on each other's news, but can I please ask you three questions?'

'Of course.'

'Are you seeing anyone at the moment?'

'No, I'm not.'

'Do you still hold a candle for Leila?'

'No, I don't.'

'Would you come on a date with me one night? A proper date?'

She could hear the smile in his voice as he answered.

'I'd love to, Sylvie.'

She came back out to Mill. 'He said yes.'

'Of course he did.'

'What do you mean "of course he did"?'

'I told him when he rang last week that if he messed you around again, I'd kill him.'

'You didn't.'

'I did. That's what families are for, isn't it? To look out for each other? Now, hurry up or we'll be late.'

The phenomenal bestseller from
MONICA McINERNEY

Those Faraday Girls

As a child, Maggie Faraday grew up in a lively, unconventional household in Tasmania, with her young mother, four very different aunts and eccentric grandfather. With her mother often away, all four aunts took turns looking after her – until, just a few weeks before Maggie's sixth birthday, a shocking event changed everything.

Twenty years on, Maggie is living alone in New York City when a surprise visit from her grandfather brings a revelation and a proposition to reunite the family. As the Faradays gather in Ireland, Maggie begins to realise that the women she thought she knew so intimately all have something to hide . . .

Those Faraday Girls is a rich and complex story full of warmth, humour and unforgettable women. Spanning several countries and thirty years, it is a deeply moving novel about family secrets and lies – and how the memories that bind us together can also keep us apart.

'A story that's impossible to put down'
Woman's Day

'McInerney is Australia's answer to Maeve Binchy,
a modern-day Jane Austen'
Sun Herald

'A delicious, heartfelt and utterly engrossing drama'
Australian Women's Weekly

'It's an almost sinful pleasure to delve into anything written by
Monica McInerney, whose delightful prose brings her rich characters
to sparkling life. This particular tale deals with how the Faraday family
confronts its secrets and, oh, what secrets there are'
Irish American Post, USA

Family Baggage

Tour guide Harriet Turner knows all about journeys. She's arranged hundreds of them for the travel agency her family runs. But nothing has prepared her for the drama, the hilarity or the passion of the *Willoughby* tour . . .

When her foster sister Lara vanishes suddenly, Harriet is left in charge of a party of tourists on a theme tour of Devon and Cornwall. The eccentric group are fans of *Willoughby*, an English TV detective show, and can't wait to meet Patrick Shawcross, the handsome actor who played him fifteen years ago.

For Harriet, the tour turns into a different kind of journey – a journey of self-discovery. She finds herself confronting questions about her family, her childhood, and her powerful feelings for Patrick Shawcross.

And the most puzzling question of all: where is Lara?

'A book to treasure that is clever, amusing and
heart-warmingly touching'
Woman's Day

'Her books are for handbags and airports, traffic jams, railway stations
and bus stops. They make us forget the irritating details of the day . . .
Warmly written, kindly and empathetic'
Sydney Morning Herald

'A warm and intricate novel about the inner workings
of everyday families'
Madison

'The exploration of family ties that McInerney
has made her trademark'
Daily Telegraph

The Alphabet Sisters

Sisters are always there for each other – aren't they?

Anna, Bett and Carrie Quinlan were childhood singing stars – the Alphabet Sisters. As adults they haven't spoken for years. Not since Bett's fiancé left her for another sister . . .

Now Lola, their larger-than-life grandmother, summons them home for a birthday extravaganza and a surprise announcement. But just as the rifts begin to close, the Alphabet Sisters face a test none of them ever imagined.

An unforgettable story of three women who learn that being true to themselves means being true to each other.

'Tender and well-observed . . . there is also plenty of McInerney's
trademark wit, but have the hankies ready for this,
probably her best novel yet'
Irish Independent

'This book took my breath away'
FreshFiction.com, USA

'You'll be laughing out loud one minute and crying the next'
Cosmopolitan

'A gentle and life-affirming story. We come away feeling better about the world and, maybe, just a little more tender towards those close to us'
Sydney Morning Herald

'McInerney is a dab hand at getting her characters exactly right.
They are utterly believable, often lovable and familiar'
West Australian